WriteNight

The Anthology

COLCHESTER

*To Auntie Teresa.
Love Jo xxx*

Published by WriteNight, 2013.

www.facebook.com/groups/writenight
http://writenightcolchester.wordpress.com/
Twitter: @ColWriteNight

contact: writenight@groups.facebook.com

The authors assert the right to be identified as the authors of this work. Individual Copyright © rests with the authors as detailed on the next page.

ISBN: 978-1 291-38268-6

Printed by www.Lulu.com
Lulu ID: 13680829

Contents

Introduction	Emma Kittle	p. 5
Camulodunum	Varun Khetarpal	p. 7
Secret History	Will Watson	p. 8
Spinning in Circles	Sue Dawes	p. 13
Park Life	Phaedra Bishop	p. 18
The Dream	Colin Murugiah	p. 22
Charlotte	Annie Bell	p. 29
The Once and Future City	Doug Smith	p. 36
Living with Grandma	Emma Kittle	p. 42
The Water Tower	Ivan Lewis	p. 46
Hannah	Jean Akam	p. 54
PT Jump	Edmund Ngai	p. 59
The Devil's Delicate Firebrand Darling	Sioux Jordan	p. 65
A Recollection	Ben Scott	p. 70
A Peaceful Place	Emma Chesters	p. 73
Isaac Palfrey	Jim Cooper	p. 78
The Great Colchester Trolley Chariot Race	Dominic Sheppard	p. 89
Patina and Palimpsest	Tom Graves	p. 94

INTRODUCTION

WriteNight formed after a group of us got together at 15 Queen Street in Colchester to write our novels for National Novel Writing Month in November 2011. At the end of a month of write-ins we decided we enjoyed having a place to write and share ideas with other local writers.

It was productive opening year - from picking a name on the first night, to writing flash fiction, sharing our writing activities, inspirations and own stories. WriteNight has become a popular, welcoming and supportive group.

This is our first anthology. We hope you enjoy the mix of genres and forms, the theme being the town in which we meet and most of us live - Colchester.

Many thanks to all the members who have entertained us with their story-telling this year, and especially to Annie Bell, Phaedra Bishop, Sue Dawes and Doug Smith for all their editing work.

Emma Kittle

CAMULODUNUM

Varun Khetarpal

Are you the place where this all begins?
The fortress of the god of war,
from where Cunobelin sows his sins,
before the Romans seize the shore.
They claim you as their capital,
a town they think invincible
'til vengeance comes to burn you down,
a Celtic queen without a crown.
With slaves and sweat comes resurrection -
Saxon, Danish, Norman, Christian;
another war, an interregnum,
your castle stormed by Parliamentarians.
So now your soldiers fight abroad
with guns and planes, these modern swords.

A SECRET HISTORY

Will Watson

The traffic lights had been red for at least ten minutes and showed no sign of changing. I sighed and tapped my fingernails against the back of the empty seat in front of me, keeping time with the rain. The inside of the bus was uncomfortably cold, despite the muggy heat outside.

"In a hurry?" the old man sitting next to me said. "When I was your age I used to hate riding in buses; sitting and waiting with no way to make the thing go any faster." He smiled to himself and crossed his fingers together on top of the walking cane he held. The cane was made of polished black wood with a silver handle, which looked something like a lion's head; I never got a clear look at it. It was the only thing about the old man which seemed well taken care of; his grey suit and shoes were expensive but threadbare and his face bore three days of white stubble. He was clean though, and smelled strongly of soap.

"Not particularly," I replied. "Just going shopping. Foul weather eh?" He ignored the question and stared through me for a moment, as though I'd said something truly thought provoking.

"How long have you lived here then?" he said, eyeing me from behind thick horn-rimmed glasses. "You don't sound local."

"Just over a year now," I replied. "I moved here to be closer to London." He kept staring at me in silence, until I realized he wanted me to keep going. "It's a nice enough town and just the right size for me. I didn't think I'd enjoy living in the city even if I could afford it."

"Have you visited the castle yet?" The bus lurched forward as he spoke. "What did you think of it?" His voice was clear and strong, out of place with his failing body.

"I have, yes, in the first week after I moved in actually. I'm not normally that keen on history, but it was interesting."

"It's Camelot you know," he said it as though he was commenting on the weather. "Camulodunum, Britain's oldest town.

You know, this town should have been England's capital, but the damn powers that be took care of that. Could I have a moment of your time young man?"

"Uhhh," I said.

"Good, now listen closely. Camulodunum means Fortress of Camulos, who was a British god of war. When the Romans arrived, they chose this site for that reason. They built their temple here not, as you probably think, to worship the emperor Claudius but to take control of the ley line which runs directly between this town and Rome itself."

"Really?" I said, resigning myself to the lecture. He'd seemed pleasant as well. Outside the rain was growing heavier, the sky darker. I'd probably have felt worried if the old man wasn't head, shoulders and chest shorter than me and as frail looking as a cobweb.

"Oh, certainly. You'll have learned all about Queen Boudicca up at the castle, but what you won't have learned is that it was actually the Welsh druids who incited her revolt." A roll of thunder swept over the town at the mention of the word 'druids', as though the sky was playing along with him.

"Why exactly?" I said.

"They needed this place," he said, his voice dropping to a conspiratorial whisper, "because it's the only place in the country where they could practice their rites just right. Human sacrifice, contact with ghosts and who knows what else."

"That sounds horrible," I said. "By the way, we haven't been introduced. I'm David." I offered him my hand, hoping that he'd be distracted from his fantasy. No such luck; he gave my hand a feeble shake, his skin icy cold and his grip as weak as a thin sheet of ice.

"John Black, it's a pleasure," he said. "And it was horrible. More horrible than a young man can probably imagine. The Romans killed Boudicca and put a stop to it but as soon as they left it all started up again. You probably think of Arthur as a good Christian king but that's not true at all. He built his capital here and invited witches and sorcerers from all across Europe to gather here; Merlin was the greatest but he wasn't the only one." He finally paused for breath, glancing around as though he couldn't believe he'd just said what he'd said.

"You could write a book about all this," I proffered. "People would pay to hear your ideas even if they didn't believe you."

"Oh I have, I have," John said. "I'll send you a copy if you like" he pulled a phone from his pocket; a shiny bar of black plastic which seemed completely out of place in such an old man's hand. I gave him my details, groaning inwardly but knowing there was no way out. I didn't have the heart to tell him where to get off and he didn't look like his heart could take the shock.

"There," he said. "Thank you. Camelot fell of course, when Arthur's magicians turned on each other. The magical tradition never ended though, and it's been carried on in secret to this day."

"And are you part of it?" I said.

"I've dabbled, of course," John replied. "But I'm not part of their coven, nor will I ever be. They call themselves the Illuminated Order of the Scarlet Raiment, bloody stupid name in my opinion. When I was a boy there were only three witches anywhere in Essex, but there must be over a hundred now."

"Could I join if I wanted to?" Maybe that would scare him off, I thought. "Heck, how do you know I'm not one already?"

"You don't smell like it," he replied, tapping the side of his nose and giving me a stern look. "I wouldn't have taken this bus if you did. You've heard of Matthew Hopkins of course."

"Can't say I have," I said, and the annoyance must have shown in my voice, because the old man's face fell. He stared at me for a second, then knotted his fist even tighter around the cane and went on.

"The witch finder general," he said. "Sixteen twenty 'til sixteen forty-seven. He was set to root up the witches by a group I believe to have been a division of the Knights Templar. They wanted to take the ley line for themselves and chose the worst possible tool for the job." I opened my mouth to tell him that this was too much, but he cut me off at once.

"Listen man, for God's sake, listen!" The old man leaned in closer and clasped his hand to mine, pinning it to the seating rail. I could have pulled away easily but the look in his eyes held me fast. It was a look of fevered sincerity which pleaded to be taken seriously.

"Hopkins was drowned as a witch himself. They'll tell you otherwise but that's a flat lie. He probably caught three real witches, out of the three hundred people he murdered," his voice was shaking now, his hand as well. "But he never came close to catching the ones who mattered." He trailed off and closed his eyes, as though he were trying to get up the courage to say what came next. The bus pulled up.

"And they're still around?" I prompted. "These witches and druids?"

"Yes," the old man croaked. "Yes they are. You believe me don't you?" I tried to interrupt, searching for something, anything, to say that would let him down gently. He cut across me, tears starting to dance at the corner of his eyes.

"Twinkle twinkle little star," he groaned. "Written right here, half a mile from us. Don't you know who the morning star is? They're out there and one day, one day they'll rule Britain again unless we stop them!"

Suddenly he noticed something reflected in the window behind me and the voice died in his throat. A man had just boarded the bus; a man wearing a scarlet raincoat over a dark red suit, water dripping from his golden-red beard. John squeaked with fright and turned towards me, so that the man in red couldn't see his face.

"Help me?" he whimpered, reaching up to ring the stop button as he did. "And I'll reward you."

Without speaking I offered him my arm and helped him out of the seat. Even with his stick he had trouble walking. He muttered under his breath as we passed the red man, who smiled benevolently at me. I couldn't make out anything John said, but it was impossible to miss how the fingers of his free hand moved, twisting through painful looking shapes and patterns.

"Are you sure you'll be all right in this rain?" the red man said. He had a rich baritone voice, and his concern seemed genuine.

"Yes," said John. "In fact, it seems to be stopping."

And just like that, it did. The moment the door slid open to let John alight, the downpour dried up and a bright ray of sunshine fell across the pavement in front of him. John turned back to me, pulled a crumpled twenty pound note from his pocket and pressed it into my hand.

"Obliged," he said, smiling. He gave the stick a quick rap on the ground and scuttled away down an alleyway, suddenly not half as frail. I went to sit back down, unable to pull my eyes away from the place he'd been.

"You don't happen to know anything about druids do you?" I asked the red man, still not properly looking at him.

"Errrrrm… Sorry, no," he replied. "Why do you ask?"

I took in the puzzled expression on a face which looked suddenly younger, saw the suit for the trendy throwback it was. He was doused in aftershave.

"Just something the old man was saying," I said, shaking my head. "Silly really, forget I mentioned it."

SPINNING IN CIRCLES

Sue Dawes

July 1994

The first time I see her, I think it is a trick. I have been woken by a nightmare so violent it causes me to sit bolt-upright in bed. I am locked in that moment between vivid dream and wakefulness, when everything and nothing is real. Two minutes ago, I imagined my new husband had his hands wrapped around my neck and was squeezing the breath from my body. I can still feel the pressure of his fingers on my skin and am convinced if I look in the mirror I will see bruises scattered above my collarbone.

I take a deep breath, close my eyes, but cannot quite shift the memory of his ragged breath and cold, dead eyes, as he applied the pressure.

David turns over, reaching out for me with heavy limbs, the rhythm of his snores interrupted.

"You all right?" he mutters, into the darkness.

I relax at the sound of his voice. My body unwinds and it feels as if something unpleasant leaves me, seeping through my pores.

I squeeze the arm David has draped over me.

"Just a bad dream," I whisper.

It is then that I see her, standing in the corner of the hotel room, next to the mahogany chest of drawers. She is young, like me but dressed from neck to ankle in a white gown. Her dark hair, under a white linen cap, looks ruffled by sleep.

I blink and she is gone, a figment of my imagination, fluttering like a moth around a flame.

All that is left is the faint smell of smoke.

I fall back to sleep.

*

July 2004

The second time I see her everything has changed. We have returned to the honeymoon suite to resuscitate a marriage that's been smothered by my husband's affairs.

Today I take in every detail: the red lion on the sign which creaks and groans in the wind, the low black-beamed ceilings, and the cracked render that looks like a battle scar. I even count the carpeted steps to the room. There are twenty-three, barely enough time to get out of breath. The last time I climbed these stairs I wore silver-strapped sandals, my heart thudding in anticipation. This time I look down at my feet, at my comfortable shoes and realise I have forgotten to shave my legs.

David opens the door to the room, and ushers me in. He does not carry me over the threshold this time, but rubs his back instead, no doubt imagining what injuries he would acquire if he attempted it. I step inside and gaze at the four-poster bed that dominates the room. It is as I remember and I rewind to our wedding night, to the passion, the discarded underwear and our hot sweaty bodies under satin sheets.

I look back at my husband filling the low doorway, and try to feel optimistic. I cannot. I want to shout at him and remind him that he was the one that punched the spark out of our marriage.

I think about our marriage as I sit on the edge of the bed, waiting for David to finish in the en suite, the late nights, the apologies and the cover-all make-up.

He gargles and spits.

"They've got the same soap," he says, though the open door.

I brush my hand over the starched counterpane. My hand touches a rose petal. Its edges are turning brown.

We trade places and I slide the bathroom lock home.

I decide to make an effort to try and remember what we had the last time we were in this room. I light the scented candles around the bath and breathe in their fragrance. I place David's razor next to the taps and turn them on. While the bath fills, I try on the new nightwear I have bought. It is sheer and silky and slips through my fingers. I look down at myself draped in transparency and see lumps that used to be curves, barely disguised. I wonder who I am kidding.

I soak in the water until it goes cold, wrap myself in the hotel's complimentary dressing gown and stick squares of toilet paper over the cuts on my legs.

David is already asleep when I emerge. I slide between the covers, hiding my relief in the pillow. I cannot do this.

Sleep does not find me. I listen to David's snores, hoping the rhythm will soothe me, but it doesn't. Each burble is like a pinch.

I reach over to turn on the bedside light.

That is when I see her again, standing in the same spot as before, as if it has been a minute, not ten long years.

This time she hovers, allowing me to see detail: the wax dripping down the candle stem onto her hand, her pale face under the white linen cap, the pattern of angry finger-prints on her neck and the blackened sleeves of her gown. She is younger than I first thought, no more than a girl.

She puts her finger to her lips. She wants me to be quiet.

And then she is gone.

*

David wakes me the following morning holding a breakfast tray. I look at the freshly squeezed orange juice and croissant, its buttery pastry shedding on the plate, but find I have no appetite.

"How much do we know about this hotel?" I ask, picking at the flakes.

"What do you mean?" he says, as he checks his hair in the mirror.

"I think it's haunted."

I see thoughts of disbelief reflected back at me, but he holds his tongue. He is trying.

"I'll find out," he says.

I use the time he is away to get dressed.

*

"They gave me this," David hands me a sheet of paper barely ten minutes later. "They were a bit reluctant. They want to know if we want to change rooms."

I take it from him. There is barely enough information on the headed paper for a text. I trace my finger along the words: Alice

Mellor, Chambermaid. Murdered in the Red Lion Hotel, 1633. Sightings in the kitchen and rooms 5 and 6.

"I saw her last night," I say.

"Here?" he asks.

I indicate where she was standing, silent in the corner.

"I've never seen a ghost," he comments, glancing at the door key in his hand.

It is something we can share.

*

That night we go to bed fully dressed. We have been to the library and sought advice from the internet. We have agreed on almost everything. David has even bought a compass. Apparently the needle will point to the direction of paranormal activity, and prove that what we see has magnetic reality.

I do not feel frightened, despite the facts: that Alice Mellor's room was sealed up for 200 years because her ghostly behaviour was so terrifying. I just feel sad that such a young life was snuffed out. And anyway she has had ample time to calm down. I should know.

We lie and wait. At one o'clock the girl has still not appeared.

"Do you think it's because I'm here?" David asks. "Maybe she doesn't like men?"

I think he is probably right. According to the reports, it was her lover; one of his kind, that killed Alice.

"Should I leave?" he asks.

For the first time in two years, I find that I want him to stay. I take his hand and slip my fingers through his. He runs his thumb over mine in a gentle caress.

"We just need to be patient," I say.

*

At two o'clock I am fighting sleep. My eye-lids droop and sag. I find I am comfortable in this silence we have found. David does not try to speak to me and I do not feel the need to reply, or stab him with accusations. We simply hold hands and wait. It makes me wonder whether we might have a future.

I close my eyes and embrace this new-found companionship. When I open them again, I see a shaft of light stabbing through the curtains. I reach over to David but find his side of the bed cold and smooth, un-rumpled by sleep.

"David?"

There is no response to my call so I switch on the bedside light, pull down my jumper, which has bunched up during the night, and get out of bed. There is something on the floor, under my feet. I look down and see drips of candle-wax. They remind me of the breadcrumbs in the story of Hansel and Gretel and I follow them through to the en suite.

The bath mat has been burnt, its edges singed but there is no smell of burning or melted fibre. I shiver, despite being fully clothed. Where is my husband?

The girl is waiting for me when I walk back into the bedroom. She beckons me with opaque fingers, wearing a smile that leaves me cold. I watch her filter through the wall to the next room. I reach over to touch the place where she has been. The flocked wallpaper is icy and unyielding.

I walk out into the carpeted corridor, and tap on the door of the room she has disappeared into. It pushes open under my knock. David is naked, spread eagled on the bed in the centre of the room, sheets tangled at his feet. I look away, feel like I am intruding and instead trace the discarded clothes that litter the floor. I listen, try to catch the sound of his deep breath but the air is silent, heavy with intention.

It is then that I notice his eyes, staring glassily at the ceiling. I step forward and pick up his wrist. It is clammy and cold and he has no pulse. There is no sign of injury, no blood or bruising. The only thing that does not belong is a white linen cap, folded in thirds on the pillow, and a compass, with its needle spinning in circles.

PARK LIFE

Phaedra Bishop

We walk through the town and then through the park, past the castle: my mum, my sister and me. I am normally last as my legs are the shortest and I am nearly always the last one out of the door and Mum or sometimes my sister stand at the front door and impatiently shout things like 'come on we're going to be late' or 'get a wriggle on' and 'come on droopy drawers'. Sometimes I feel a bit cross about this because I don't really mind about being late, it seems to me like we are late all the time and nothing ever really happens about it and so I don't see why everyone is so scared about it. What is so bad about late? Sometimes I think it is like all the grown-ups (and maybe my sister who is almost grown up but not quite) are frightened of 'late' because they think it is a monster that will gobble them all up.

I also don't understand when they say about the wriggle because I haven't got anything called a wriggle to put on, some of my clothes need me to wriggle a bit to get in them, like my skinny jeans, but I think that is different. I really don't know how I would begin to put on a wriggle and even if I did have one I think it would make me slower and not faster. They even sometimes say about getting a wriggle on on school days and I am never allowed to wear my skinny jeans to school.

I really especially hate it when they call me 'droopy drawers'. If I wasn't feeling droopy to start with, I think my smile goes a bit droopy then. Maybe what they actually mean to say 'droopy jaws'? But I don't like that either.

We all head through the park as we are going to swimming lessons at Leisure World and we are late just like normal. As we go I like to look around. My favourite bit is the wall I like to clamber on (I think about the Romans who must have clambered on it gazillions of years ago and I like that probably Boudicca even clambered a bit here once).

Another favourite bit is the playground that I sometimes go to play in and also I like walking past the big group of TEENAGERS who wear long black coats and dye their hair, some have it purple or red or blue but most have it black; to match their clothes I expect. I walk past them and when I do the best bit of all is staring at them. Sometimes I try to pick on one to stare at in particular and I think that they think that they look scary and I stare at them so they have to start thinking that maybe they're not scary because there is a seven year old girl, who is in the park on her own, who is not at all scared by them.

So those are my favourite park bits.

*

We walk through the park almost every day and we are normally so hurried that we don't stop to enjoy it properly. A friend told me the other day that our very own park won the Alan Titchmarsh 'Best Park of the Year' award in 2010 -quite an impressive accolade- and I was too preoccupied even to notice! Occasionally I admire the lovely gardens, or how glorious the Virginia Creeper growing up the side of the museum is looking, and I guess I do appreciate the bird song sometimes. However, if I am honest, most of the time I don't notice these things as I am too busy thinking about the myriad of tasks and chores there are that I need to have done but have not yet achieved. There are bills to be paid, meals to be prepared, letters to post, jobs to apply for, birthday presents to be purchased, phone calls to be made and all sorts of everyday ordinary things which somehow magically need to be squeezed into not enough hours a day.

Several dozen times a week, we make our way through the park-sometimes we are going to town, but we walk through on the way to and from school, and when we have to go to the swimming pool. The most frustrating thing is that no matter what time of day you can be sure I will have to stop at least three times and chivvy along Lois who seems to love nothing better than being on a permanent 'go slow'. This is particularly concerning when the park seems to be frequented, increasingly these days, by those dreadful looking youngsters who insist on loitering about by the benches near to the gates.

*

I've been trying to pin point when exactly it was that my mother transformed from being 'the most wonderful lady in the world' to 'okay' to 'the most embarrassing freakazoid who ever walked the earth'. Take the other day for example, it was a normal kind of our family 'stressy' leave the house. It was the usual thing, mum running late and faffing around with her hair and stuffing toast in her mouth while simultaneously trying to apply lipstick, change her shoes and feed the cat and then discovering she can't find her keys. She always decides that the moment she is ready (which is always about ten minutes after we were supposed to leave) that we have to go that very instant and then, unless Lois and me are standing right by the front door she does that thing when she pretends to be patient and 'okay' but anyone can see that she is angry as dynamite inside. All it would take would be for me to say 'uh, did you know there's marmalade in your hair?' or Lois to say 'your new perfume smells a bit like cat food,' and man, the whole house would go up in fireworks - only they wouldn't be pretty.

It was one of these 'normal' days and mother had a right stress on. I was trying to help, but you know, on days like that mum won't be helped, so I just stood there and eventually we were all walking up the road, down the High street and then taking a left into the park. Mum was talking on her mobile and I was rehearsing in my head what I would say to the swimming teacher to explain why it was we were late again and hoping that if I practised it over and over in my mind I might be able to come up with something quite witty and smart. Anyway, I was eager to get there 'cos nothing close to smart or even vaguely witty was occurring to me and so I was walking pretty fast. I hate being late. It is so embarrassing. But not nearly as embarrassing as this...

Before I knew it I could hear a full on screaming fit from a voice I knew only too well. No, not Lois, but mother dearest. I could've died of embarrassment: one minute we were walking through the park thinking about swimming and the next there was my mum going apoplectic at one of the Goths who hang out in the park. OMG! What the hell did she think she was doing? How dare she do this to me? I turned round and there she was having a full on ranting fit at the tall one who wears the full length leather trench coat. Mum had kind of transformed and was wagging her finger at him and making ridiculous vitriolic threats, a fountain of saliva was spattering out of her mouth as she shouted and screeched something like '…ever attempt to intimidate my darling daughter...' I've heard of people wanting a hole in the ground to open up but man, I promise you that if aliens had descended from Mars in that moment and said 'hey kid - us or your psycho mum - make your mind up,' - I would have happily and willingly opted for the rest of my life as an alien captive. Tbh, I was really worried that someone from that crowd might recognise me and make my life hell-on-earth. I checked the sky but there didn't seem to be any aliens coming forth to rescue me… there was nothing for it, I was going to have to just make my way to swimming on my own- and maybe, just maybe, I'd make it on time.

As I took one look back at the scene in the park, before I scarpered round the corner and out of sight, I could see them, both Mum and Lois, who was still rooted to the spot. The Goth looked almost as embarrassed as I was feeling, he stood there with colour rising through his whitened cheeks and his mouth hanging open, aghast. Mum's lipstick was definitely smudged by now, and she had hold of Lois' hand. She was tugging at her, trying to get her to move, saying 'time for a wriggle on – we'll definitely be late' in that potential fireworks tone she has. And this was the oddest thing: Lois didn't seem to care at all. She just stood there, rooted to the spot, staring at the Goth kid as he began to slink away. Just staring and staring and staring.

THE DREAM

Colin Murugiah

The howl of the 'Mediterranean Wolf' was as pitiful as those of a stuck pig. Another twist and ligaments creaked. He was deaf to his victim's cries, the gut-wrenching squealing, the moans of a man too broken to cuss. He reached for the poker.

God's will was being done. Scarred lips twisted as he stirred the coals; the zealots believed it, the ignorant believed it; part of him believed it, but if he was an instrument of the divine, it was by convenience. He would have the location of the chamber out of him or by God, he would crush every bone, muscle and sinew.

"It is the will of God," he breathed, leaning in as he raised the now-white tip.

*

As she returned to herself, Janie caught a glimpse of brilliant orange against hard, scarred features, a broken nose and a broad black-rimmed hat and robes.

Someone called her name. She sat back with a gasp. Colchester Castle's walls felt solid and cold against her back, the damp creeping through the seat of her jeans. The chisel pressed up from her back pocket; involuntarily, she winced, shifting.

"Janie! Janie, come quick; you've got to see this! We've found it–"

A blur filled her vision; wavy black hair, olive features. "Tony?" That was not the face she'd seen, raw green eyes, dark cropped hair... 'T. Isaacs' the name tag read. Dirty, blue overalls, ragged, torn. Musty gloves. Five o'clock shadow; excitement twinkling in a chocolate-brown gaze that missed nothing. That face, not his face, only... was it?

"Whoa, what happened to you?" Strong fingers found her chin. His eyes never strayed to the shimmering waters; she lost herself in that stare. "...You didn't drink from it? Tell me you– God, what were you thinking–"

She shook him off and rose unsteadily, a lingering after-taste of smoke clinging in her mind. "You found it?"

"Yeah. Listen, are you sure you're–"

"I'm fine." She glanced around the floodlit chamber. "They're real... the knights." Effigies cast from life; stone swords and armours: their excavation had carried them beneath the well, to another, older level, then cut across and up. They'd followed the drains, the rusted ladder... a sealed chamber. For a moment, she'd seen spiralling stairs, a perfect mosaic, medieval frescos, pointed Norman arches, drapes. Gold leaf, reds, blues, whites; untouched by time. A shrine. The vellum tome lay open, as colourful as the walls. Candles, thicker than her arm, stood unlit; censers, still bearing incense, suspended between the knights. The pool rippled gently around the isle's pedestal, its muted light dancing with shadows.

Now the chamber was grey, lifeless. All that remained was the waters' crystalline glow. But Tony was more excited about the hoard. Roman silver, buried when the old temple of Claudius burned down. He hadn't seen, couldn't see.

"It's everything we imagined!"

She gazed into his face, through him, past him, at the shadows, at the knights, their coat of arms faded, worn. An alcove lay beyond; beside it, a tunnel, an afterthought, forgotten. "He was here?"

"Who?" Tony demanded, fidgeting. "Come on! Twelve Amphorae!"

Shaking her head, she brushed him aside and bent to peer at the wolf sigil. Embossed on the stylised kite shield, remnants of silver and black glistened. Latin letting sat beneath it. "I need to go."

"You're crazy!" His hands spoke louder than words.

"Don't drink it." Her foot found the first rung. She gestured to the wolf's inscription. "It's cursed."

*

Arthur FitzCole, the Mediterranean Wolf. The book slid from her fingers. Had he escaped? She turned to the massed tomes, the online miniatures, parish records... a red-headed witch hunter. Scarred lips. A glass eye, crazed. It spoke to her. Words unformed, soundless.

Recognition in the blue; light, sky-grey, intense, her own. She had seen it that afternoon, in the pool, in the olive-green stare, through the hate, the agony... a face not her own. It wasn't hers, it wasn't. But the angle of those cheeks, the arch of the brow, that nose; her own, unscarred, unbroken, yet slanted just so... A dream. Nothing more.

The miniature stared back at her. In its endless gaze was Judgement. Her finger slammed on the mouse. William Jacques, 1613-1667, May his soul burn in Hell forever. Drowned. Hesitation held her; unwillingly, she entered her search. The ancestry of Jacqueline, starting with her grandmother. Coincidence. It had to be. What the hell was going on here?

Normandy. Two hours of research pointed to Normandy. Feuding families. Saxon land. Fiefs. How long could a grudge last? A vendetta of absurd proportions? Across centuries? She had to know more.

*

Death would come quietly. A heretic must confess before his or her soul could be purged. Sin must be cleansed with fire, lest the fires of damnation burn forever. The perfect pretext; the heretic knights were gone. Their last bastard descendant would join the rest.

She sat up with a start. Her handbag clattered from the desk; the phone was ringing. Twinkle, Twinkle, Little Star...

Rubbing her elbow, she rose shakily. "Tony? Yeah – no, I'm fine. When? Sure. Yeah, I fell asleep – no, I needed to get up. Seven then? Okay. Bye for now."

The phone dropped softly onto the open page. His face stared up at her. Rough black lines on faded yellow. A flash. "Tony...?" Her eyes darted to the text.

[— Sry mk it 8? —]

*

She shivered. The breeze wrapped around her as she drew her coat taut; it was August, not April, and the weather couldn't decide which. Gusts, light showers, and sunshine, all mixed together. A chill tore through the trees, and they bowed, leaves desperate to hold on. Clouding over, the skies wept a half tear; November perpetual, despite the greenery. Her gaze lowered to the tombstone in front of her. The lettering was worn, the crest still present. 1617-1671. Manningtree's noose hung empty after all. Relief squeezed her throat painfully. The light was fading but there were still a few more hours. Her woollen glove cupped the rim, forefinger tracing the inscription. Latin, again. She looked up, then left the dead in peace. If only their ghosts would leave her alone...

*

"Didn't think you'd mind."

In smile's façade, Janie's lips pressed tight. Skinny denims drew stares and loose cotton breathed; Tony was oblivious.

"How nice to see you again, dear." Lemon sweetness met thinly veiled disdain. A slender white hand with sparkly nails patted his forearm. How nice she found the time to volunteer as a curator and still work as a psychiatrist. Clarissa de Grâce. On and on, he prattled about details. Neither rolled her eyes.

"Shall we order?" Clarissa's fingers stroked the webbing above his thumb. The blonde's grey gaze lifted, her glistening lips parting. "Something sweet?" The wine menu found itself in his hand. Bored suggestions followed. He never noticed, head bobbing as he considered each of the whites. "A chardonnay?"

"Pollock?" Switching menus, Clarissa ended the debate effortlessly. Champagne. To celebrate. And Tony even let her talk him into not paying for it; her treat.

Stomach clenching, Janie forced herself to smile back. She should have thought of it herself; if it wouldn't have broken her bank... Abruptly, she realised her teeth hurt and reached for her water. Opposite her, the other woman lazily lifted her own in mimicry; she didn't even have the courtesy to offer a small shrug but watched over its rim. Stay the hell out of my head.

"Hake."

"...Scallops? With garlic mushrooms?"

"If you like," Clarissa sniffed slightly, smoothing her gown's slit as her knees crossed; Janie decided it was a good thing black was slimming. She instantly felt ashamed, but the thought savagely persisted, threatening further slurs. Clarissa's glance, following a final indifferent scan of the desserts, did nothing to discourage it. Black Forest Gâteau? To share?"

Tony's first attempt to attract a waiter failed. So did his second and third. As he rose, she smiled up at him, "Good day at the office?"

"Hmm? Oh, yeah. Clarissa reckons – well, you tell her, Clar."

"Tell her what, darling?"

"The pieces. The amphorae."

"Ah."

"They're worth a fortune! Just like we thought!"

Like you thought. Janie wondered how he could be so blind; realisation dawned with a thigh's flash. Matching... she smiled sweetly as she reached for her wine. "That's great. How much?" She didn't care.

"We already have a buyer interested! The museum doubled its offer. They must really want them."

A row of sequins; their suggestion not even a promise, and heads turned to mush? What the hell was wrong with him? She shouldn't have worn jeans.

*

"Callisto?" Janie repeated listlessly. The empty air offered no answers. It didn't need to. Mediterranean Wolf. The translation tore at her. Why did he have to smile? She said it like it didn't matter. What was wrong with him? So what if their next dig was in Normandy; why did he have to bring it up? Anyone could see Clarissa wasn't laughing with him. No one knew what it meant, the significance. Tony 'Callisto' Isaacs...

Unwillingly, her eyes were drawn to the statue; unblinking, it stared back, judging. Guilt's pang warred, tugging at her already knotted insides. She shouldn't be here. Her reflection agreed, rippling as her feet dangled precariously close to the edge. At home, she couldn't get away from the photos. The sites they worked littered the walls with memories she couldn't bear. She thought about the park and the swings, just her and the moonlight, but their creak grated and all she could think of was his voice. The graveyard was too exposed, too creepy, even for her, and offered no answers. He cared more about Saxon spears and Norman steel than tapestries and sandals, ancient battles, not bones. Now the only bones that mattered were those marked with war. What happened to real history? It wasn't about the kings and princes; it was about everyone's lives coming together, piecing the puzzle. It didn't matter if a royal tapestry cost as much as a warship. 'Their stories and ours.' His words. His smile.

Unwillingly her gaze stared through itself, the shimmering doppelgänger fading to dancing light and stone. A shiver took hold; the damp chill defied sun and stars, time and seasons.

She had to know. With cupped hands, she sipped from the pool again.

*

[— Wher R U? —]

The cool water trickled down her lip. It tasted... metallic; acrid sweet. No, that wasn't it. Her tongue flicked out and stole the last of it. She shivered.

With a hiss, the phone juddered. The screen flashed blue and died. Her fingertip traced its on-off button and dug in. It didn't like it down here. A flicker, and it flared to life. 05:00. Half a bar left. Two hours since her last check.

Another text.

[— U wer mnt 2 b here 30 mins ago. —]

Hesitation held her. A swallow caught her throat.

[— Im sry —]

Shaking too hard, her finger refused to send it. The screen died.

*

The bottle slid from her hand. Green, cloudy, cracked... silver flashing, liquid pooling; timeless, perfect stillness. It shattered. A blur; then an oval drew sharply into focus. Olive features, cropped black hair; another fading face in the crowd. As daylight pierced through her pounding lids, the whispering rain washed her and the concrete verge. Such simple relief; lips too cracked and parched to question their balm's purity. She swallowed. The caked bile stung her mouth and throat anew.

Queen Street's ever-present stench seeped beyond her nostrils, beyond care. He had gone anyway. That half-smiling vixen hanging off his arm, her black heels and sequins... no mention of her part, or the chamber. He said he needed her. That last text that never came through, not until it was too late. Twelve amphorae. Twelve fucking amphorae. They had worked together eight years...

She forced her eyes to stay open. Through hazy thoughts, and falling mist, clarity touched her. Straightening her crumpled shirt, she rose above the lap of pungent vomit, the shoe splashed by some stranger's piss, the last night's foray into the clubs.

Admiration stung more than lust. Why didn't he look at her that way? Why hadn't he waited? Twenty minutes. She missed him by twenty minutes. After she had finally crawled out the well's under croft, the castle entrance was deserted. Looking all over the park revealed nothing beyond skittish squirrels and a hissing goose. A half crumpled Snickers had kept it at bay while she made her rout up the hill. Her socks and the ankles of her jeans joined the generous grass as they shared their sopping payload, slowing her enough to take pause. There, through the peeking clouds, dawn broke. Then as now, the sun glinted, sparkling as the drizzle waned. She shook out her jeans. She finally understood.

It was time to end the feud. Her pace quickened; two steps ahead, he froze. She met Tony Callisto's backward glance with a smile...

The Mediterranean Wolf would howl.

CHARLOTTE

Annie Bell

"Hurry up!" My sister laughed. I removed a stone from my shoe as the bright sun warmed my shoulders. A few steps on, I caught her up. She had stopped rather abruptly and was staring intently to her right. I folded my arms and shivered a little despite the warm weather.

"That wood," Hollie whispered nervously, pointing towards the boundary of a grove, edged with sweet chestnut leaves. "Something is pushing me to go in."

"Let's have a look," I replied.

Curious, we scaled the barbed wire fence, tiptoeing tentatively into the damp wood. What would we find? Mosquitoes buzzed, flickering, as their wings reflected the dappled sunlight. Young saplings mingled strangely with the corpses of once great trees. Dead sticks cracked and snapped beneath our feet. I followed as a strange presence guided Hollie on a winding route between the trees. Without warning, she stopped. In front of her was a deep hollow in the ground.

"Something's wrong," she grimaced.

"Where are we?" I asked. Hollie checked the map on her phone.

"What's Charlotte's Grove?" she enquired. Her words struck me to my core as a memory flickered in my mind.

"Let's go," I muttered.

"Why?" she quizzed.

"I'll tell you in a minute." Scrambling through the trees, we clambered back over the barbed wire fence, emerging breathless into the sunshine.

"What happened Jo?"

"Charlotte. My teacher told us about her at school."

*

I remembered many things. A sketchy black and white photograph depicted a dingy scene. Two majestic trees with exposed roots stood eerily - like undead kings - by a stagnant pool.

"This, year 6, is Charlotte's pool." Mr Stimson announced. "Charlotte's father, who owned Berechurch Hall, loved her very much. He built the pool for her in Lethe Grove. It is said that she may have drowned there and her ghost still walks near the pool."

That night, horrified, I recounted the tale to my parents. How could there be a ghost so close to my home? Desperate to calm me down and despite their beliefs, Mum and Dad told me not to be so silly.

"There's no such thing as ghosts," they reassured me. I was pacified but the story never left me.

*

That afternoon, after I dropped Hollie home, I was curious. I decided to investigate the truth about Charlotte's life. She had to be more than just a ghost story.

I headed straight for Colchester Library. As I began my research, uneasiness taunted me. I quickly discovered recorded sightings of Charlotte's ghost. A poem told me of one lady's peaceful and friendly encounter with Charlotte, near to her pool. As I absorbed this, I felt suddenly cold again. It felt like someone was watching me but the presence did not feel evil.

Switching from ghosts to more concrete facts, I soon found out that her father – Sir George Henry Smyth – was the Bob Russell of his time – a long standing MP, representing Colchester. It seemed he really did adore her. She was his only child and he built a pool for her, which was inspired by a tapestry that hung in the library of Berechurch Hall.

As I read about Charlotte's life, I felt someone stroke my hair and shoulder affectionately. I turned around but there was no-one behind me.

From what I read, I gained the impression that Charlotte was a wonderful, loving lady, who commanded great affection from all who knew her. I knew then that I had nothing to fear from Charlotte but I wanted to know more.

The following morning, driving my Mum into Colchester, rain threatened. Approaching Tenpenny Hill in Thorrington, I spoke about my research.

"Do you remember Charlotte's pool?"

"Of course," Mum chuckled. "Why?"

"I've been researching Charlotte," I explained.

"How come?"

"I want to write her story."

"What brought that on?"

"Yesterday, Hollie and I accidentally found the site of Charlotte's Pool, in the grove where her father had it built – just down Cherry Tree Lane."

"No! Where we used to walk the dog?"

"Yes – exactly! Afterwards, I went to the library and found out that she was called Charlotte Smyth, although her married name was White."

"OK. Go on," Mum was intrigued.

"Oh Mum. It was so weird. As I was researching, someone stroked my hair. I think she was there."

"She probably was." Mum can, in fact, sense ghosts, so she wasn't surprised. "What did you find out?"

"I saw a picture of her pool. It was beautiful – decorated with shells and a huge marble tablet emblazoned with the word 'CHARLOTTE'."

"Her Dad must have loved her to build that," Mum replied.

"I know. I can just imagine her sinking into the water, attended by maids, warming her feet on the red brick floor - really luxurious. I read about her ghost too. There have been loads of sightings; Charlotte – The Lady in White."

"Ooh. Scary," Mum giggled.

"Actually, no. She's ..." I stopped abruptly. The hairs on my neck stood to attention.

"She's here," Mum confirmed my feeling. In a situation like that, there is only one thing to do.

"Hello Charlotte!" we both chorused. Although I couldn't hear her, I knew she could hear me.

As we entered Alresford, I decided to ask her a question.

"Charlotte, would you mind if I wrote your story?"

"She just giggled – a shy giggle," chuckled Mum. "How did I hear that?"

"She approves then?" I smiled. "In the encounters I've read about, she always instills a sense of peace. She seems lovely, doesn't she?"

"Yes, she does. I'm getting a warm feeling from her."

"I'm glad. When I was a kid, Mr Stimson made her seem really scary. I was -"

"She doesn't like that," Mum interrupted. With those words, the chill pushed aggressively through me. The car swerved violently. I fought to regain control.

"Sorry, Charlotte," I gasped, breathless. Panic gripped me. My body shook. "I didn't know. He may not have told it how I described. You remember being eleven, don't you, Charlotte? At that age, all ghosts are terrifying. Of course, I don't think that now." Charlotte's anger receded.

"She's having a little think," said Mum "In the back. What else did you find out?"

I accelerated onto Clingoe Hill.

"She married on her nineteenth birthday."

"How romantic!"

"It was, wasn't it? They were enormous party animals as well. Dances at Berechurch Hall went on 'til five in the morning!"

"Really?"

"Yeah. I read about one in the Standard – for her father's fiftieth. Apparently, everything went wrong after Charlotte betrayed her husband. No-one knows what she did but it seems he forgave her and gave her a beautiful white gown edged with swan's down as a token of forgiveness. She couldn't forgive herself though and walked, tormented, through the halls and grounds of Berechurch Hall day and night."

"Poor girl!"

"They moved to Wethersfield in the early 1840s but she died in 1845 from consumption. She was only thirty three and left six young kids."

"That's sad."

"Yeah." I stopped at East Gates, waiting for the train to cross. "I think she was helping me, Mum; finding the information was a bit too easy. Mum?" I glanced around. Mum's face seemed tired, greyish and vacant. I wondered what was wrong and nudged her.

"Sorry," she muttered. "Charlotte, I have to ask you to leave for now. Come again though."

I parked at St Botolph's. As we passed the Dickens Hotel, umbrellas in hand, I could feel that Charlotte remained with us.

"Are you coming for a girly shopping trip?" I joked but it wasn't funny. Outside Franklin's, Mum stopped, clutching her chest.

"Charlotte," she commanded. "You are not welcome here. Leave now."

"Has she gone?" I put my arm around Mum's shoulders.

"Yes. I didn't want to do that but she wouldn't go. She was making me feel dreadful."

Half an hour later, drinking tea in the Art Café, the colour returned to Mum's cheeks. We didn't mention Charlotte again until we were with someone who would know what to do.

That Friday, Mum, Hollie and I went to the Castle Pub for our friend Sioux's birthday. Being psychic clairvoyant, we hoped she might be able to help.

"Happy Birthday, Sioux." Mum beamed. "Did Jo explain what happened?"

"Not exactly. Tell me." Mum told Sioux everything. As if on cue, Mum's face paled. Charlotte had returned. Sioux placed her hand over Mum's heart. Heat poured from it, re-energising her.

Sioux explained that Charlotte, being earthbound, was acting as a psychic energy vampire. Not having passed over, she had no energy source and therefore, with no malice intended, drew energy from anyone who would let her.

"She is friendly, isn't she?" I asked.

"Yes," replied Sioux hesitantly. "But she says she was murdered." My heart sank. I knew Charlotte had died young but murder had never crossed my mind.

"What does she look like?" I enquired.

"Long hair, young face and she's wearing a white dress – like a nightdress." Sioux replied. This matched the descriptions I had read. "She says it's not what she'd normally wear out and about."

I began to explain what had happened when I talked about Mr Stimson.

"Don't aggravate her," Mum begged.

At that moment, Mum slumped. Sioux stood up abruptly, beckoning.

"Right. Come here, Charlotte." Hollie and I assisted Mum, following Sioux into the ladies. I was curious what she would do.

In the ladies, Sioux closed her eyes. She prayed for the obstacles impeding Charlotte's passage to the other side to be removed.

Sioux relayed the conversation, which ensued between her and Charlotte.

"Charlotte," she announced. "You are not wanted in this family. You have no connection to them. Leave them alone."

Charlotte replied, "Yes. I know. It's just that no-one's ever bothered before. People seek me to glimpse a ghost but they never try to talk to me." I felt sad. Charlotte had been trapped, completely alone for nearly 170 years. Sioux listened awhile.

"She misled me. She wasn't murdered," Sioux announced. "She was angry with her family for leaving her alone for all these years. Before her death, Charlotte was seriously ill. She had a high temperature and begged her Dad to take her back to Berechurch Hall and put her in the pool. He did as she asked but the icy water worsened her illness. Her Dad was devastated and rushed her back to Wethersfield but she died soon after." Sioux's tone altered.

"Charlotte," she commanded. "Go into the light. Go to your family." Charlotte was afraid that her beloved father – full of guilt for his role in her death – would not be there. She resisted, shoving Sioux about violently.

Charlotte asked Sioux, "Will Jo write my story?"

Sioux responded, "Yes." Struggling, thrown about increasingly forcefully, Sioux boomed, "CHARLOTTE. YOU – MUST – GO." Mum visualised a light and Hollie noted a shadowy outline of a figure behind Sioux. As the figure disappeared, Sioux's body sagged. She prayed.

"Oh holy Lord, our Father. Please take Charlotte into your care and seal the door to keep her safe." Finally, she had gone into the light.

Over the next fortnight, I wrote Charlotte's story. As I sat with Mum, typing, I felt my hair being stroked again.

"I have to make this a bit spooky, don't I?" I asked Mum, "to engage people." Charlotte was no longer taking energy from anyone. As we sat there, she simply gave us, as the stories described, a sense of love and peace.

Mum chuckled. "Charlotte's talking to me. 'I'm not spooky.' That's what she just said. She's laughing!"

*

Epilogue

It was done. Sioux had enabled Charlotte to cross over. I had written her story. There remained just one more task. I knew Charlotte was buried at St Michael's Church but the location of her grave had eluded me.

The day before Charlotte's birthday, Sioux, Hollie and I entered the Audley Chapel. As I pushed open the stiff door, the cool air within contrasted with the sunny afternoon.

"There she is." I announced. Indescribably beautiful, Charlotte's effigy in white marble reclined beneath two hovering angels. I placed a bunch of pink roses – Charlotte's favourite flower – before her monument. The sculpture and epitaph confirmed what we already knew. Charlotte was a wonderful lady, struck down tragically. I cannot vouch for the revelations given by her spirit but I can vouch for her kindness and sense of humour. Silently, we absorbed the words.

"In the vault beneath rests all that yet is mortal of CHARLOTTE. The beloved wife of Thomas White Esq of Weathersfield, the very dear and only child and heiress of Sir G.H. Smyth, Bart of Berechurch Hall. She died Oct 17th 1845, aged 33 years.

"This tablet is erected by her sorrowing relatives, to mark the early tomb of one who as daughter, wife and mother, combined with a most tender affection, the exemplary discharge of every duty, and the practice of all Christian virtues.

"These words may serve indeed to tell the stranger how much lamented was the loss of one, so lovely in her life, and yet so early doomed; but alas! No epitaph can fitly record those endearing qualities which have raised for her a sweet and lasting monument in the hearts that once shared her love or rejoiced in her friendship."

As we left, we knew. Charlotte was finally at peace.

THE ONCE AND FUTURE CITY

Doug Smith

Banks got the call around 6.00am, just before the end of his shift. It was Aiken.

"Need a second man in the interview room, sir," he said in his young, estuary accent. "And I wanted to be extra careful anyway. There's something not quite right about this guy."

"Fine," said Banks. "What's he done?"

"Breaking and entering. The Jumbo tower, actually." Banks heard a rustle of paper as Aiken checked his notes. "And he attempted suicide."

"I'm on my way down."

He found Aiken waiting for him outside the door of room two. Banks raised his eyebrows. "Shouldn't we have a counsellor in on this one?"

"They don't start 'til eight."

"Can't we wait?"

"Not sure we can," said Aiken. "He's insisting on speaking to someone right now. Getting quite agitated."

Banks sighed and shook his head as he buttoned up his suit. "All right, I'll play Freud for a while. Let's get on with it."

Aiken pumped the handle of the door hard so that it made a loud clunk and then swung it open sharply. A man wearing plain black clothes jumped up from the table, his chair scraping backwards on the floor behind him.

"Mr Porter?" said Aiken, as if nothing had happened. "Please, sit down. We're here to take your statement."

Banks shut the door quietly. Porter glanced at them both with anxious eyes and then pulled the chair back to the table. There was a few days' worth of stubble on his face, dark hairs flecked with grey.

Aiken sat down opposite him. Banks pulled a chair from the corner and then reached over to press a switch on the interview recorder.

"Thursday 26th September 2013," said Banks. "D.I. Banks and D.S. Aiken taking a statement from Mr…" He checked the notes again. "Julius Porter."

"OK," said Aiken. "Mr Porter, you were detained just after 1.00am this morning in Balkerne Gardens, where it was found you had forced locks on the fence and maintenance doorway at the Jumbo Tower. Officers also restrained you from climbing out of a window in the top room, after you had shouted your intention to kill yourself." He looked up at Porter. "You have declined legal counsel. There was something more you wanted to tell us?"

Porter ignored Aiken and looked at the recorder. "Is that thing switched on? Is it recording?"

"Yes, and yes," said Banks.

"You might want to turn it off."

"Why?"

"Because what I have to say will sound insane. Unbelievable. Or, if you do believe it, the implications will be too big for you people to understand."

Banks smiled. "It's a legal requirement," he said. "And I'll take the risk."

Porter looked nervously from one policeman to the other, then dropped his eyes to the table and picked at a groove on the surface. "All right," he said. "This will sound very far-fetched to you, but I am a time traveller. I am from the year 2092."

Aiken snorted a quick laugh and then there was silence for a few seconds. Porter looked up and Banks held his gaze.

"Go on," said Banks.

If Porter was joking, he wasn't showing it. "I am a professor at the Colchester City University of Sciences. We developed a means of temporal travel in 2089. Since then, we have been experimenting with short trips to interesting points in history."

Aiken laughed again. "This is priceless. So what are you doing in 2013?"

Porter's jaw clenched and he looked down at the table again. "I had no choice. I'm not meant to be here. But then neither are you."

"How's that?" said Aiken.

Porter hesitated, scowling at them. "It's a long story."

Banks spread his hands. "We're here to listen."

Porter straightened up in his chair and took a deep breath. "Myself and a colleague travelled back to 60AD. We wanted to witness the birth of the Golden Age of Roman Britain, when King Prasutagus died. That was when Suetonius Paulinus, the governor, defeated the druids on the Isle Of Mona and rushed back to Anglia to meet Boudicca and her daughters when he heard the news. We thought we would join that journey."

"What are you talking about?" said Aiken. "Boudicca fought the Romans!"

Porter glared at him. "Yes, yes, I have found out about your version of history. Trust me, things turned out very differently where I come from.

"Paulinus knew very well the King was ill and didn't have long to live. Also, he had no sons, which made him vulnerable. When the message came, Paulinus raced across Britain to Venta Icenorum to offer Boudicca his sympathy and make a deal with her."

Porter leaned back, as if relaxing into his subject. "He was an intelligent man. Prasutagus had left his land and wealth to be shared equally between his daughters and Rome, to make sure his legacy would continue in peace. So, Paulinus set up a ceremony where he became co-ruler with the elder daughter, whom he also married, and thus made himself the most powerful man in Britain. Within two years, he had united the lands of the Iceni, the Trinovantes and the Catuvellauni, and within ten, all of Britain and Wales as far north as Carlisle, with Colchester as the capital.

"Their Romano-Iceni royal line lasted until the Viking invasions, but Colchester carried on as a strong and popular city. It grew enormously later, as all capitals did. Much bigger than Rome. Bigger even than Bucharest, in my time."

Banks rubbed his chin. "So why aren't we living in this city now?"

"Something went wrong." Porter closed his eyes, pinched the bridge of his nose and sighed heavily. "Oh, all right. We, being the fools we were, changed history!" He shouted the last few words and punched the desk. The recorder rattled.

"Oi, oi! Calm down!" said Aiken. "We don't want to have to get officers down here."

"Just carry on, please," said Banks.

Porter turned sideways in his chair, staring at the wall. "Stupidly, my colleague and I arrived at night. The lights from our vehicle startled the druidic people, and they thought the Romans had a new weapon. They attacked again much more fiercely at daybreak, and when the message arrived, Paulinus and his men could not leave for Anglia.

"So, the local garrison took matters into their own hands with Boudicca. A few days later, Paulinus received a message that they had ordered her to be flogged and had raped her daughters. He was furious. This had wrecked his plan, but he couldn't run back because the druid attacks were still strong.

"Eventually more messengers came, reporting that Boudicca had amassed an army and the Iceni were rebelling. The small local Roman forces were easily beaten and Colchester was destroyed. Paulinus finally beat the barbarians at Mona and immediately marched south with his army, aiming to intercept the tribes-people before they reached Londinium. He was too late, of course.

"We realised we had to get back to our time and assess things, quickly. But my colleague was captured by druids and killed. They thought he was a Roman spy. I managed to escape and made it to where we had hidden our craft."

Porter took a deep breath. "But something was wrong. The time-travel device wouldn't work properly. Our time-line no longer existed, and I couldn't get a fix on anything. The first time-jump landed me in 1743. I tried again and ended up in 2013. Then that was it, the device failed and I was stuck."

Porter went back to picking at the table. "I was still in north-west Gwynedd, of course. The power packs were nearly depleted, so I decided to drive somewhere familiar, to Colchester."

"Drive?" said Banks.

"Yes, we installed the device in a car." Porter stopped and looked up at them again. "You know the old saying, 'All roads lead to Colchester'?"

"Not really," said Aiken.

"Of course not. It has no meaning to you. When I finally made it here along one of your dangerous, curvy, criss-cross roads, I couldn't believe what it was like. The Greater Dunmow estates, just open fields. Coggeshall should be full of elegant Victorian town-houses, with the shopping mile stretching along East and West

Streets, but it's just a village... No sign of Theatreland and Lexden Circus. Where did it all go? How could it have never even existed?" He put his head in his hands and started shaking it slowly.

"Obviously, you're upset about something," said Banks.

"Damn right," spat Porter. "So would you be if you'd destroyed two thousand years of history and replaced it with this." His voice caught in his throat.

Aiken butted in. "Just say we do believe you -"

"And I fully believe you don't."

"Well, let's assume I do for a second. Where is your time-machine now?" Aiken didn't even try to suppress his smile.

"A car park, by a section of Roman wall. Priory Street, you call it."

"I would have thought someone would have noticed something," said Banks.

"I said our device was in a car," said Porter. "It doesn't look so different to one of yours."

Aiken stood up. "Let's go and find it then."

"Interview terminated," said Banks. "06.55." He clicked a button on the recorder.

"I'll be needing my keys," said Porter. "And my boots."

They took an unmarked car and headed out. Porter stared blankly up Balkerne Hill as they curved their way around the Southway roundabout and then burst into tears. Banks turned around to ask what was wrong.

"You cut straight into the Cathedral mount," said Porter. "Took a chunk out of it, just like that, for a road. You have no idea what a magnificent place it could have been."

"Sorry..." Banks faced front again as Aiken turned up Head Street.

Porter carried on regardless. "Or the rest of Colchester. Sheepen - the financial centre for all of Europe. The twin Universities of Sciences and the Arts that face each other across the Colne. The vast docks that stretch from Hythe to Alresford Creek and the beautiful sweep of the Brightling Suspension Bridge. A whole city, all gone."

"It's never been a city," said Banks. "Britain's oldest town, though."

"We did apply for city status," said Aiken. "But Chelmsford got it instead."

"A small, old town that should have been a mighty city," muttered Porter. "So sad."

They turned in to the car park. Aiken left the car at an awkward angle by the pay-and-display machine.

"Where is it then?" said Banks.

"There," said Porter, nodding. A squat, rounded silver vehicle sat in a space near a corner. Behind it loomed the end of the old bus garage. "I should check the quantum core, it may have become unstable. Could be dangerous."

"Really?" said Aiken.

"Yes. Do you have my keys?"

"I do," said Banks. He watched Porter unlock the car and then took them back.

"Just to be safe, would you both stand behind your car?" said Porter. "Don't worry, I'm not going anywhere. I only wish I could."

Aiken looked at Banks, who nodded briefly.

"OK," said Aiken. "But we'll be ready."

"Of course."

They retreated, watching Porter. He glanced at them, reached inside the car, fiddled with something and then stood up again slowly.

"Thanks for your help, officers," he said, without turning round.

There was an intense flash, and the 'whoomph' of a heavy implosion. Banks instinctively shielded Aiken's head with one arm as they ducked down, eyes closed.

After a minute, the rain of vaporized metal and glass stopped falling onto the tarmac and cars around them. Banks stood up and slowly walked to where Porter's car had been. One side of his face felt sore and the back of his hand glowed scarlet with deep sunburn. Alarms sounded in the distance.

In the pile of ash and debris stood Porter's boots, looking strangely as good as new. Banks picked one up and found the foot still inside, unscathed. The rest of Porter was gone.

LIVING WITH GRANDMA

Emma Kittle

Mum was going through a tough time. Divorcing my dad and with two girls to look after. It played havoc with her nerves, or so she says. That's how I ended up with Grandma and Grandpa. At first for a while, and then for good. We lived in a bungalow on St. John's, two bedrooms, not a great deal of space.

As I grew so did the washing pile. One day my grandmother made a new rule. "You can only put washing in the bin on Tuesdays and Thursdays. No other day of the week. Is that clear?"

"Yes, Grandma." I was not really bothered about the rule. It made no difference to me. I just accepted her ways, and put my washing in the bin on Tuesdays and Thursdays. Sometimes I had to think about which day of the week it was and return to my room with an armful of washing. I hid it in the bottom of my wardrobe, until it was a washing day. Sometimes I forgot and the pile in my wardrobe grew, too big to put in all in one go, so it had to be shared out amongst the next few washing days.

It was early one Sunday morning when I realised that Johnny Ashton was going to be at school with the boys' school band, on Monday, and that all of a sudden it was important that I wore my best blouse.

"No washing until Tuesday!" my grandmother barked. "You know the rules!" I took the blouse back to my room and began to sweat when I thought of seeing Johnny Ashton whilst wearing the other one, particularly as I'd be on show at the piano. As I sat on my wobbly bed, on the itchy welsh blanket, and leant back against the wall, through the window I saw my grandmother talking to Mike Freeman whilst pruning her roses in the front garden.

I took my chance and crept over the plastic floor rug in the kitchen to the cupboard where she kept the washing powder and took a cupful, locking myself in the bathroom with it. Pleased as punch, I washed the blouse myself in the warm water of the avocado sink, enjoying the silky transparent cotton sliding over my hands.

I rinsed and wrung the blouse, rolled it up and put it in my bag for church. It was the only thing I could think of to do. As my grandparents conversed with Pru Richards and Angela Stanton at the entrance, I wandered innocently around the back to where the sun shone on the grave of Harvey March. It dried my blouse nicely while we sang 'One More Step' and took our communion. When I went to pay my respects to Great Aunt Jeannie, I marvelled at the crisp white blouse and thanked Mr March while I was at it.

And so, along with the fabric of my teenage existence, came a mission to clean and dry without being caught. The rules of my grandmother's home were obeyed and life on the surface was orderly and uncomplicated. Life underneath was okay too.

One day I was sitting right at the very front of Biology when Lucy Arnold knocked on the door. When invited to come in, she asked that I go to Mrs Woolcroft's office immediately.

Of course, the entire school was scared witless of Mrs Woolcroft, and I was no exception. Her black gown billowed through the corridors as free as her white hair was taut. Girls froze with straight backs, hoping they weren't breaking an unknown rule as she passed.

I followed Lucy down these corridors, the oak panelled walls and parquet floors dimly reflecting the lights high above.

"Sit here," she said as we arrived outside the office bearing Mrs Woolcroft's name. I'd never been this far down this corridor before. I'd only got as far as Mr Diamond's door and that was when he congratulated us for doing so well in the hockey tournament against St. Anne's.

It was lucky that I soon heard 'enter' because if it had been a long wait I might have become even more agitated. As it was, when I tried to turn the brass door handle, it slipped through my sweaty palm and I couldn't get a grip. I had to pull my cardigan over one hand and use the other to turn it. As I did I went from the darkness into light and had to squint.

When I found my sight again I was surprised to see my grandmother and grandfather sitting before her, Grandma upright with box bag on her knee, Grandpa hunched and avoiding my gaze. Sparrows before a hawk.

"Patricia Moore."

I wasn't before royalty, and it was the 1980s not the 1950s, but I replied, "Yes Maam".

"Can you explain this?" Before her was a pile of white powder, and for a moment I had no idea how to explain it.

I looked at my grandparents, avoiding my gaze, and back at Mrs Woolcroft, eyes burning into my gaze, then at the white powder and then at the small floral bag sitting beside it. It was my washing powder.

I was embarrassed for them. I wondered what they thought their granddaughter was doing with the powder hidden at the back of her underwear drawer. (Along with that note Johnny Ashton sent me, I just remembered). I did think, for a moment; why did you look in my drawer? I felt the frustration of having nowhere, no place of my own. A small well of lava formed in my stomach.

But when I saw his head hanging low, I didn't feel betrayed. I pitied them. I saw how old they were, how helpless they might feel in this job thrust upon them.

"It's your washing powder," I said. "Smell it." It was a type that my grandma bought, from Jacks. A surplus store, with big bags of washing powder. Barely a scent, not like the perfumed kind that my friends smelt of, but it was there. Why didn't she recognise it herself?

My grandma's body drooped, the rigid wrinkles dropped. "It's just we'd heard the stories," she was saying to Mrs Woolcroft. "The ones in the Gazette, about the kids and the heroin and cocaine, even in the playground. We heard and we tried to ignore the stories. And then when we saw the bag it was all we could think of. And when I asked Mike Freeman, he said it was unusual for a girl of your age to spend so much time in her room." She wasn't looking at me.

The pity was leaving my body. The well in my stomach began to swirl. She carried on, "And the sneaking around the churchyard. Even Pru Richards noticed. She was the one who asked where you were. And we couldn't tell her."

Mrs Woolcroft was nodding in affirmation. Grandma was feeling more understood. The lava was whirling and growing, in places burning my ribs. "And when Angela Stanton said it was unusual for a girl to spend so much time running water in the bathroom, we really didn't know what to do." The lava began to bubble, bursting and spitting and burning as it travelled into my throat.

And then my headmistress said, "There's nothing to worry about here Mrs Moore. Our girls don't get involved in drugs. Now if you don't mind, we have lessons to be getting on with, and the piano concert with the boy's school band to prepare for."

I watched her scurrying to stand. Heard his sigh of dissatisfaction.

I held open the heavy oak door, the brass sphere smooth in my grip. They passed through, him raising his brow, her looking straight ahead.

The lava settled and cooled. But a hard crust formed around the edges.

THE WATER TOWER

Ivan Lewis

An Elephant parade was what it took, a picture card full of trailing elephants walking in a chain and a single word – 'Jumbo'. The treasure box fell from a tangled heap where no-one ever saw fit to look. Abilene discovered the card inside with a poem written around the edge and printed at the top right hand corner, almost smudged, was the word 'Colchester'. This particular box was lozenge shaped, full of fur and hidden well away from any casual viewer's attention. Within the collection she had selected a grey card, separate from the other items examined. Many of the other decorative objects inside, she surmised, must have been left here out of pure caprice.

The scene in the picture looked foreign and washed out of all colour; "how could that be so?" She wondered – "why resort to greyscale imaging rather than a more usual colour wash?"

Her tribe had forgotten there was an 'up here' in the hay trap so it was easier for Abilene's mind to roam abroad, away from concerns over survival which had become everyone's currency. While she puzzled out the box's contents, the girl was wholly aware she could remain unnoticed for more than a while.

Abilene and her twin sister Abby were both orphans. But what did they care? Their embryos had been manufactured from raw materials, but most other children her age were human born. Growing infants via chemical processes had been the fad not so very long ago but the practice had since been abolished because of the radiation hazard drifting on from area to area, making the job now entirely worthless. No birthing process could be trusted to work properly without the priority accorded from human supervision.

The picture on the card made Abilene remember something – something she ought to have sensed from the manner of the scene. Elephant paper chains were clever, granted – a real blast certainly. Also the photo showed a crowd looking on as if they appeared out from the foamy dust, standing side-bound cheering along both road curbs. She had never seen the like before in her life.

Granted, elephants that talked were a made up creature straight from the fairy tale shift at bedtime. She knew exactly the tale about Jumbo, the elephant battered by a deserting knight, or somebody resembling a swordsman whose destiny was to marry a princess. Unfortunately the princess was too busy having something called a romance. Abilene didn't know what having a romance entailed but hoped it was something nice. She had later learned the truth in that Jumbo had been mortally wounded, run over by a steam train – in comparison this more mundane version of events was disappointing. 'Jumbo Juggernaut', she remembered, once spun water from a large tube protruding from his head, technically known as a trunk. The silk worm grew thread in a similar fashion. Many such fairy tales she had encountered included golden spinning wheels bedecked with fair maidens operated like spinning tops.

The weather never really changed as far as Abilene was concerned. The endlessly hot days seemed impersonal, a general thing, incapable of clemency allowed by the silver streaming cast up in the sky. As was usual, the early morning brought about a blanket grey settling overhead, a pale arena for loneliness where nobody would walk or become intimate with anyone else. The silence above translated itself amongst the landscape furniture, composed of dead tree trunks bolted to the ground; threaded fences heralded silent houses with shadows popping through the holes where the windows used to be.

On her later travels around the locale, Abilene thought very hard upon matters surrounding the picture card she had recently found. Some of her nightmares had grown from preoccupation with this one thing – though much nicer meditations were coming round, she was certain. She imagined herself a queen sitting on her antique oaken throne; she watched the nearby river run along at its most pedestrian speed. Later she knew it would gather in size and greet the sea through large chunks of land sliced away. Over this river came the aqueduct, a vast frame astride the valley near where Abilene's camp lay in session. Many shapes through the mist were tangled up in the structure, some more discernible, others not so recognisable. Watching the superstructure – iron wrought with spaghetti like entanglements in the design - made the bridge seem older than it was – perhaps similar to a cathedral, ornate with spires and buttresses repeated along the valley floor. She had seen something similar in an old book discarded in the general wreckage outside the village.

Abilene sat on the overlooking point where the false trees stood nodding up on their fake peak. Certain shapes became alive in her mind and took on the guise of strange animals or creatures folded upon themselves and delicate – it reminded her of origami she had learned from her nurse when much younger. Her rather sardonic temperament had made for stubbornness at lesson time. The nurse took offence when Abilene laughed at the rather pointless fare offered in the name of education – she did not wish to learn about marrying anyone. So after all enthusiasm spent, they resorted to origami once the curtains were drawn at dusk. Here on the aqueduct, a particular shape looked like the mighty stag beetle but it couldn't be that, perhaps a peacock instead. Abilene wondered what genius may have folded those creatures, manipulating the materials like clay between lubricated hands.

On one memorable occasion, the nurse had smote her quite vigorously for arranging five words she had provided into innuendo expected from a much older girl. Abilene was not sorry and made matters worse by throwing her work on the floor. All was lost, or so it seemed. Eventually, this tyrannical dowager grew sickly – then took herself to bed where she contemplated flu like symptoms without actually suffering the complaint in full. Maybe it was Abilene she was escaping, although Abilene didn't trouble herself further on the matter. She was a free spirit, unlike her other playmates who were much more compliant in nature. So she had to make her own breakfast while the old crone was supposedly dying upstairs on a simple canvas camp bed, reserved for the lower vassals, who disliked serving her even more than Abilene herself. It was a harsh reality that the house rules did not provide adequate accommodation for the formulaic pecking order of the lower staff – or for that matter the wild yard cats, most of which resorted to sleeping in Abilene's room next door.

Her thoughts ran on like these self-same wild cats, with a spring in their step, and then came a triumph in suggestion: there had been inside talk of an elephant type statue nearby in a patch, a jungle which once came with a large cast of other beasts, reputed as being fantastical and incandescent. They said it was not designed on a real living elephant. Everyone knew real elephants were extinct and adverse environmental conditions were quickly blamed. They were then entombed inside ancient books and molten readouts from the old discarded computer terminals her guardians kept ready for backup. Was this the same Jumbo Juggernaut reworked from the multiple images she saw on the picture card or did it seem contrary to these ideas? Abilene needed to find out for herself – maybe bring evidence back to camp, even soothe her nurse with the news, in the hope it would motivate her out of bed and earn Abilene a treat. If she was to truly allay the adult's doubts, she had better take the snapper just in case a realistic picture was required. She believed being young was something that brought on a less cynical approach to life's delicacies; being old required greater circumspection.

There was no going back after she crept into the back yard. She stopped to smile at the sky full with sun - a rare sight - and then stole the gadgets needed for recording the monument on arrival. It would be a night's hike for sure. Travelling through the night, distinct from the fiery day's crest, two lost children would move in the oblique shadow, the shade of day. She had made poor Petrioc oblige her by shouting at him. He brought her a lamp, lit with single tallow, enough to avoid it blowing out completely in the darkness.

Abilene was sorry she hadn't listened more closely to the adults chatting between work sessions because she was unable to piece together a reliable map that would lead her away from the known leagues, her homeland by the southern estuary. Admittedly, much of what people talked about now was about the northern slopes where a fortress had once been built. All she was allowed were orders for supper and instructions on actuating the cleaning roster.

In the picture card, she could see the cardboard people were leaning from windows and the crowd cheered the procession on as if it was the last thing they would ever see. Some people were mysteriously looking round at the camera towards some kind of fourth wall. With all that waving and cheering – Abilene wished she could be just as sonorous, excited and joyous as they were; unfortunately a long epoch separated her from those regaling the elephants depicted on the card.

Night turned into day and at last, Abilene knew she might have found her quarry. Every which way Abilene swung the camera, there was no real logic pointing it at the sky like a telescope. For nothing save the clouds filled the sky, nevertheless there was a glint of something new up there – a reference evading viewpoint. The motivation for waiting had passed and some of the clouds had swum out of sight through the covering mist. Overhead grew some trees but many had become withered and ceased to hold the enfolding canopy. Years before today's excursion, a jungle had dominated the surface area covering the eastern zone of the island coast.

It was obvious the watchers would be favoured by a more changeable sky, redolent from a time when it was perfectly ordinary for twitches in the weather cycle to form occasional talking points amongst strangers. Unfortunately circumstances had led to a more permanent cloud cover, virtually impregnable to any sort of weather system, high or low.

Sitting on an immediate plot was a giant arching structure, onerously high, the likes of which looked strange to Abilene. For her, it resembled some monolithic creature basking under the cloud cover, a world away from when it was built. Abilene with a camera and Petrioc with his binoculars, they watched from below on the asphalt island surrounding the tower. Abilene gasped - at last Jumbo had come into view, a similar contraption to the aqueduct though the arches were far less numerous.

She grew tired and felt increasingly dispirited walking around the total devastation lapped up against the tower, the only salient exposition in the unbroken landscape. Upon looking, the horizon was filled by no other nest of triangulation than the very tower itself. But to Abilene's dismay the monument did not neatly resemble the elephants in the postcard; just a casual similarity remained. It might have been possibly left behind by civil engineers derived from a race of people who had died out quite needlessly – she was not quite sure. Of course all the real animals were alive once upon a time.

If one was to mask their feelings like Abilene did, mostly out of grief, or cover up their motives for awarding this enormous thing a higher ranking among life's mysteries, she was left to only guess at the function performed by the masonry which had cause to make up this giant superstructure. Legs had been built from floor to sky, intense with brick, supported by an inner apparatus reworked as a long shaft. The shaft led up to what looked like a Mastaba tomb perched on top. Four sides had been positioned to form tall rounded arches. Four corner piers fashioned like elephant feet seemed frozen alive.

Abilene noted a sloping roof plonked on board the stout frame - red brick upon brick piled up to the high viewing gallery. A person looking on might drown in such a herculean sight above but there was an intricate red gate below, where visitors could gain access at the base of the structure.

After she had a chance to reflect on the scene, the air was filled with the sound of Petrioc's much softer voice.

"Why have you brought me here? It's a ruin, like those cemeteries you once told me about – places where dead people get buried underground."

"You mean the mausoleums," she replied.

"The very same, thing – marble angels and such, except I cannot see any round here," the boy remembered.

She had spoken to him, being of a younger age than her own, about centuries past, and about ready-made legends and stories, half remembered, retold with magic in the eye. Books read, on her own, though words were not generally recognised by her familiars known to have ages of older franchise.

There was a suggestion that they would both climb up the shaft until they could witness the view up on top. Like the elephant picture card had exited from a camera's mechanism, she hoped she could make a similar stamp capturing the final scene overlooking what was purely desolation.

Presently, both children climbed a red cast iron spiral staircase until it came high enough to see the waste lands spreading out indefinitely. The tower's innards were rusty and the larger spaces Abilene observed might have once served as a container ample in size. On the viewing platform, giant holes formed row upon row in perfect circles – the red plugs, covering the holes, stood open wide. Industrial nuts holding the seals in place had in fact fallen off, probably dilated from the heat. Abilene looked inside each gap and wondered if they served exactly like the spherical objects meant to stop water flowing away, or maybe they were a contrivance for drawing water from some underground spring. Above the giant torso, this creature had big teeth too, long ones under the thick roof. Later she looked back out from the same flared gaps found gashed into the masonry over all four sides.

At the approach to the apex, the two found that there was one last windy chamber forming the pinnacle section of the structure –

similar to a lantern on a lighthouse. Nothing compared with the awe Abilene felt for her forebear's handy work, having ventured this far up in the statue without the fear or regret expected. Inside the lookout room the light was at its strongest, the shadows were at their darkest, everything was at their extreme parameter. She knelt on the floor and curiously she remembered the most important thing in her life – the days when she was in her happiest state – moreover the people from those very dreams. From horizon to horizon, the dying sun, a red giant, lit the tiny room with a mixture conjoined: fire and dust thrown up in the late glare of the gleaming orb.

How did she lose something so precious and forget so completely? "My sister," she thought, "the red haired girl, my kindly adoring sister – the separation had made me despair; since then I have become a mute witness – I forgot how beautiful you really were."

Strangers had fostered both Abilene and sister Abby at birth then took one baby away from camp – the mother was merely a birthing conduit. Abilene was left bereft, because her new guardians felt loneliness was of better service in life than growing up with younger siblings in tow – they felt isolation promised more wisdom. Sister Abby knew the power of laughter. Laughter, Abby believed, was the best way to nurture solace – great and lasting friendships won in the wink of an eye, the turn of a dress, the lightness in the step, comparing the way one looked, dressing up poppets – all these pleasures shared with her twin long ago made Abilene's thoughts acrobat over and over, and on to much happier ground, although ever so briefly.

"Oh Abby where art thou now you silly princess?"

"Dead", she replied.

"How?"

"I drowned – murdered, strange as it may seem."

"Who?"

"The people who took me away didn't want me anymore. I did leave you a note in that old box you found within our secret hiding place."

Petrioc threw a rock over the catchment but the crash fell silent. The stone had failed to cancel the enchantment produced in the whistle of the wind or more especially, her reluctance to ever leave the spot since Abilene had discovered what had been lost in time.

One single eye from Abilene's pair produced a prism shaped tear large enough for gravity's hold - it flowered through a stream of sunlight and spread into all the different colours ever known, extracted from the spectrum according to natural law.

Shattered in the middle of the floor was a corroded metal cross baring the insignia: N, S, E, and W – a tired weather vane discarded. Abilene pulled out from the other junk: an object, shaped like a broad sword, illuminated by the sunlight reflected. She wielded it in mid-air. And along the blade there stood a golden elephant still shining, with the trunk stretched out in front. Designed like a badge, the shape was identical to the elephants shown on the black and white card. It existed in silhouette on the blade edge, not too big, not too small – very thin.

"Is this what she meant?" Abilene mused. She reread Abby's note around the card's length:

"Oh torch of day, up there it lay;
Though by taking away our golden top;
In exchange for those deep less spangled gifts;
We watch our image reflected in the stars;
So once more if one could steal a look at this heavenly spot;
Or watch the arch of a rainbow drop;
Then hope will soon recover, new life revealed
An elephant never forgets."

HANNAH

Jean Akam

Hannah came into my life in 2000. When I say came into my life, I do not mean physically, although at times it has felt like that as she became a force to reckon with - especially when she wanted to be noticed. That year I had a request from a relative of mine who helps people with information about family trees. He asked me if I could go to Colchester Record Office to do some research for Evelyn, an American lady who had contacted him. I agreed and began to research an ancestor of hers, one Hannah Delight.

I found an entry in the parish records of St. Giles Church, a church now closed but one which had been built around AD 1150 on part of St. John's Abbey Cemetery. The entry said '27th January 1787 Hannah Ann, natural daughter of Rebekah Moss'. I almost freaked out when a 'voice' in my head said: "You have found me!"

From that moment on, Hannah became a presence in my life. I asked the assistant in the record office what the words 'natural daughter' meant and was told it meant the child was illegitimate. No father was mentioned. However, later I found a marriage entry of a Michael Delight who married a Rebecca in St. Giles Church on 20th August 1789 when Hannah would have been about 20 months old. The entry for Hannah's birth lists her mother as 'Rebekah' not 'Rebecca' but the different spellings may have been down to the parish clerk at the time, as they entered the names in the parish records.

Eighteen months before I had the request to research Hannah, a parcel was wrongly delivered to my house, when it should have been delivered to the same number in the road round the corner from me. I took the parcel to the right address and met an American lady on holiday in Colchester with her husband. I thought no more of it until a thank you for finding Hannah email from Evelyn turned into an on-going email friendship. She later became my E Mom after my Mother died. Then one day, attached to an email, was a photo of Evelyn and her husband outside The Foresters Pub, in Castle Road.

All I could do was sit and stare at it in disbelief, as Evelyn who had requested a search for Hannah, was the same lady I had delivered the parcel to, which had been wrongly delivered to my house.

Even though Hannah was born in 1787, she could have lived now as her life according to the parish records was similar to a lot of people living in poverty today. I will let a resume of the vestry minutes of St. Runwalds Church, 1818 to 1929, do the talking for me. These details follow on from a paper I read in the Record Office stating that Hannah's Brother, William Delight, had gone to the parish to ask them not to charge Hannah parish rates as she could not afford them.

Feb. 19, 1822	Hannah's poor rate is lowered.
Mar. 29, 1822	Hannah must have complained about the new rate as the churchwardens decided her rate should remain the same until the next meeting.
June. 6, 1822	Church wardens recommend that Hannah attend the meeting of the new rates, as they believe the rate is no higher than others in similar situations in the parish.
Feb. 1823	Settlement examination of Hannah Delight, where she tells of being born in St. Giles parish and that her father was born there. (I believe that the marriage of her Mother, Rebecca, to Michael Delight, in 1789 and the mention that her father was born in the parish of St. Giles, may prove that Michael was Hannah's birth father.)
Feb. 26, 1823	Examination when Hannah Delight Moss names William Fincham as the father of her child.
Dec. 11, 1823	William Fincham to be summoned for the "whole of his pay".
Jan. 21, 1824	William Fincham is to be apprehended and committed if he doesn't pay what he owes to the parish.
July 7, 1824	Hannah Delight Moss is summoned for non-payment of poor rates
Oct. 7, 1824	William Fincham is to be summoned for monies owed to the parish.

Dec. 8, 1824	A warrant is issued for Hannah Delight for non-payment of poor rates. (The Poor Rates, at this time, were the responsibility of each parish and intended to help the poor and needy. When Hannah was summoned for non-payment, perhaps she was trying to prove she was too poor to pay them?)
Feb. 3, 1825	William Delight brings "action of law" regarding the church officers action of taking Hannah Delight's foods (goods) from her house for payment of her poor rates.
Feb. 11, 1833	Hannah apparently loses her child to the father, after church officers deny support for her child and the father "agrees to take it free of any charge upon the parish."

Hannah remained with me for a few years and sometimes caused mayhem. I have a good memory and never forgot my front door key until one day, when it was pouring with rain, I returned from the town to find I did not have my key. I had no way of getting in my house until the evening and wondered what to do. All of a sudden I heard a voice say "go to the library" - the voice of Hannah. At first I thought I was imagining the 'voice' but it kept repeating "go to the library". I felt very angry as I had lots to do and did not need this interruption to my day. However, I had two options, either to get very wet or to keep dry in the library, where I could at least read the newspapers.

Cursing the 'voice' in my head I went to the library as instructed and busied myself in the reference section, where I appeared to be 'guided' to a book on marriages. On opening the book, the first thing I saw was Cornelius Delight, a landlord of a public house in Priory Street, followed by other Delight records, perhaps Hannah showing me her family? Sadly there was no mention of Hannah but I could feel her presence. I also discovered that the name Delight was derived from the Dutch name Deloitte and may have meant that Hannah's forebears had come over with the Dutch weavers, but that is just conjecture, I found no proof. My anger turned to a feeling of being grateful to Hannah for guiding me to this information and I was amazed at her determination to guide me in the right direction.

The last time, prior to this, that I felt Hannah's presence was one Monday morning during a meeting of Act V at the Mercury Theatre. Act V is a group of people aged 50 plus who meet at the Mercury and undertake acting, dancing and other theatrical things. The group was given the task of taking on a character and acting the personality as they saw it. I started to wonder who to be, when a familiar voice sounded in my head. "Me, make it me," the voice said. This was followed by a loud guffaw and what could only be described as girlish giggles. Thinking I was going nuts I thought, "I know very little about the person you really were Hannah". There was a pause and then "lady of the night" was thrust into my thoughts. "OK Hannah," I thought, "I will humour you."

I was amazed at the words coming out of my mouth as I performed the part of a lady of the night called Hannah. It was like I had been taken over. I freaked one of my friends out as she said my voice changed completely and my performance as a lady of the night was praised by the tutor.

Hannah disappeared from my life as swiftly as she had entered it. In a way I missed her as I had enjoyed following her history through the records I accumulated. From the parish records I found about her, it seems Hannah had a very hard and sad life and I never found any marriage for her or came across any more children born either in or out of wedlock. I also did not find any definite work that she undertook. However, she lived in the Brewers Arms, (the owner of which was a Charles Cobbold who also owned a brewery down North Hill), and the pub building was situated in what was the so called red light district in Colchester, so she may well have earned a living as a prostitute. This again is conjecture as I have no proof, but she was ideally situated if she was and had a room in which to entertain men. In the early part of the 19th century, the area around the Brewers Arms had quite a few pubs and girls were allowed to ply their trade with men by the landlords.

Before 1793, soldiers had been billeted in the town in public houses but with the advent of the Great French War it was decided to build a barracks in Colchester to accommodate the soldiers. Churchmen in the town started to get worried about the increase in prostitution which helped to spread sexually transmitted diseases throughout the town. The whole situation became worse when the Beer House Act (1830) allowed pubs to open for 18 hours a day. The soldiers had to turn for comfort to the arms of prostitutes, as they were not allowed to marry unless they asked their commanding officers' permission, plus there was a lack of accommodation for wives and families before the barracks were built.

Hannah has intrigued me ever since she came into my life and I would love to find out what happened to her, but this may never happen. However, one of her descendants, Evelyn, the American lady I met, has enriched my life in many ways. Hannah's eldest son in spite of the stigma of illegitimacy did well for himself and became respectable. He was John Samuel Burton Delight who became a master tailor in London and was also a beadle in a church there. A beadle was a lay assistant in churches; one of the most well known being Mr. Bumble in Dickens's Oliver Twist. This John was the Great Grandfather of Evelyn. The younger son whose name I never discovered was brought up by William Fincham as ordered by the parish and I never found out what happened to him either.

I still have many unanswered questions about Hannah I would like to explore. For example, did she eventually find happiness? I hope so as she deserves some recompense for the hard life she apparently led. However, I would like to thank Hannah for bringing Evelyn, the American lady, into my life. She and I were meant to meet.

PT JUMP

Edmund Ngai

"Please explain to me how this works again professor?"

The professor looks at Andrews with a reassuring smile, "Certainly." The professor continues to strap him to the chair and begins to explain, "What we are about to do is called a PT Jump which allows you to travel in mind and body to the past for 12 hours but only within the confines of your age."

"And I can go anywhere I want and talk to anyone I want?"

"That's correct."

"Aren't you worried about paradoxes or stuff like that?"

"Detective, you're not the first person to use this machine, we have a highly advanced device called a temporal vacillation scale over here that picks up any irregularities to our time-line, so if there had been paradoxes, we would have known by now. To our research and knowledge, every action you take during your time in the past either corrects itself later or it causes an alternate reality to be created, when you come back after 12 hours nothing will have changed and everything you know about the world will still be the same. Now, any more questions?"

"Just one, are you sure this is safe?"

"Of course, there have been no fatalities since the early trials. But as a warning, just brace yourself."

He looks at the professor worriedly. "Brace myself? Why?"

"Let's just say travelling through time will be slightly painful. Here take these, it will help."

The professor feeds him a couple of dark pills. The strong aniseed taste makes him gag as it begins to linger in the back of his throat.

"How painful will this be?"

"Well each case varies. Some say it's as painful as falling down a flight of stairs."

"That's not too bad."

"Others say it's like jumping off a two storey building."

"Okay... that's quite bad."

"And in rare cases it's like being a human speed bump on the A12 during rush hour."

"Wait... what?"

"Don't worry. You are only going back 10 years and from what we have learnt, you have kept yourself in stellar condition over the years, unlike that ex-cage fighter who went back 25 years. Now, no more questions, let's get started."

The professor makes his final checks on the apparatus and initialises the first stage of the PT Jump. Andrews' body begins to numb and his eyes are fully dilating. He cannot see anything other than bright white light, his senses disappear one by one, his body is now entirely numb, the sharp chemical odour of the laboratory is no longer there, the loud machines running in the background has grown silent and the after taste of aniseed is gone. The professor flicks the final switches and the PT Jump commences.

Andrews feels weightless, floating into the ether for a few seconds then slowly feels a gradual descent. The velocity increases rapidly and he is now at a free fall. The numbness in his body starts to fade. Still completely blind and deaf, he feels the pain of every minor and major injury he has ever had, one at a time. All the punches he has ever taken in drunken fights, all the times he has stubbed his little toe in the early morning on the coffee table and especially that excruciatingly painful time where he got stabbed chasing a mugger.

Absolute agony for what seems like an eternity, when all of a sudden, the pain stops. A moment of both relief and bliss, however, this is short lived because the free fall also comes to an abrupt stop.

Finally feeling the weight of the world again, his senses slowly return to him, each part of his body aches in different ways. He adjusts to his surroundings both mentally and physically.

Lying on the floor of the old basement where the laboratory was based, he quickly realises that there is no laboratory, nor anyone in sight. He gets up off the floor and with every movement he makes he can feel the aches alleviate from his sore muscles, he shakes his body vigorously until all the pain and aches are gone. The detective slowly composes himself, checks the time and heads for the town centre.

It is refreshing for Andrews to know that despite all the changes they will make to Colchester over the next 10 years that some things just won't change. Sloppy Joe's is somehow still in existence, the High Street is never short of a road full of cars and the Castle is standing tall. He observes the people passing him by with their mobile phones and can't help but feel slightly nostalgic; he can't remember the last time he held a phone to his ear. However this is not the time to be reflective, he reminds himself why he chose to come back to this specific point in time. He has to find out why his older sister, Louise went missing. Was she murdered, abducted or did she just run away?

He has memorised every little detail that was in her old case files. Nobody close to Louise saw her after she left a lunch date with her friends. He was in school, his mother was visiting his grandparents in Ipswich at the time, his stepfather was at home looking for a new job after he had lost his old one and her friends went shopping around town. They claimed she was heading home but his stepfather said she never did make it back. There had been no reported sightings of her from the public. It was as if she just fell off the face of the earth.

Andrews goes to Louise's last known location, Café Rouge, picks up a local newspaper, sits down at an empty seat in the corner, orders a cup of tea and waits for his first glimpse of his long missing sister. He checks his watch, 12:46pm. Another 14 minutes until his sister walks through the door with her friends. As every minute passes he reminds himself to stay calm, stay patient, just watch and no matter what happens, see it through.

1:02pm, Louise and her three closest friends, enter the café. It has been 10 long years since he last saw her and now she is sitting two tables across from him. He tries to hide his elation, it takes a lot of willpower for him to stay in his seat and even more so not to shed a tear. Every little memory he has of her rushes back to him as if the floodgate that has been suppressing his memories of her has finally been opened. He watches on as she enjoys the company of her friends. He tries to analyse her behaviour, no unhappiness or any apparent signs of her wanting to run away. The group decide to leave and Louise realises she has forgotten her wallet and apologises to her friends as they pay for her lunch. She decides to go back home to retrieve her money so she can go shopping with her friends.

She walks to the bus stop only to realise that she doesn't have enough change. A young man notices, walks up to her and offers her some money for the bus fare. Andrews nonchalantly watches from a distance, extra wary of this young man, as he looks very interested in his sister, too interested. The bus arrives. Louise, the young man and the detective get on. Louise sits in one of the middle seats, the young man sits next to her and Andrews takes an empty seat at the back so that he can observe everybody on the bus. The young man strikes up a conversation with Louise and they talk for the duration of the journey. The bus reaches Louise's stop, the young man follows her off the bus, claiming it is his stop as well, but as they talk they are both oblivious to the fact that Andrews is following them.

As Louise approaches her street the young man shakes her hand and waves her off. The young man begins to walk away but pauses for a second. He takes a short glance at her walking down the empty street and follows her.

She seems anxious, she can probably sense that she is being followed. She picks up her pace but the young man catches up to her. Andrews stands cautiously at the end of the street. She turns back to recognise the young man, she faces him apprehensively. He tries to calm her down, apologises for scaring her, he explains that he wants to see her again and asks for her phone number. Louise is hesitant but she calms down and gives him a number.

Andrews realises that the number she was saying was not her own, it was familiar though and after a few seconds deliberation he recognises that it's the local takeaway's number. Unaware of the fake number, the young man apologises again and walks away. She arrives back at home safely but something doesn't add up. His stepfather stated specifically in the old case files that she never made it home.

A loud scream shrieks from within the house into the silent street. None of the neighbours are normally in their homes at this time of day. Andrews can't stand the screaming any more, he rushes into the house and sees his drunken stepfather pinning his half naked sister against the sofa. An incredible anger runs through every fibre of his being, he tackles his step-father onto the ground and punches him repeatedly until he comes out of his flash of rage and realises that his stepfather is unconscious. He gets up, takes off his jacket and puts it over his sister's half ripped blouse. He guides her outside and they walk to a small park nearby.

"Are you okay?"

Tears are streaming down her face but she begins to calm down.

"It's okay, you're safe now."

"I'm not going back, not to that house, not with him in it."

"You should report him to the police."

"I can't do that, I know this sounds stupid and I am trying so hard not to defend him... but despite what he tried to do just now, he isn't a really bad person and my little brother idolises him. If he ever found out that the person he trusts most in the world did this, I'm scared... I'm scared that he would go back to being the antisocial delinquent that he used to be after our dad died."

Andrews' knows that the main reason why he joined the police was because of his stepfather's guidance. He also knows that since the disappearance of Louise, his stepfather never touched alcohol again.

"Will you be okay?"

"I don't know, maybe."

"What are you going to do now?"

"I have a friend who moved to Liverpool last year and she came back to Colchester for the week... I'll probably go find her and see if I can stay with her."

"So that's it? You're going? Not a single word to your mum or brother?"

"I can't lie to them and they can't know the truth, not from me anyway."

"You have to let them know that you are alive at least; your brother will be devastated not knowing that you are alright."

"Maybe one day, when he is all grown up, I will send him a message to let him know I'm okay."

Andrews is relieved to hear this, but he realises that after 10 years, he still hasn't received any word from his sister. He begins to wonder and hope that she didn't commit suicide.

"Sorry to lay this all on you, but for some reason I feel comfortable around you, like family. You know, you remind me of my brother actually, but a lot older"

"Yeah I have one of those faces, always a brother, never a lover."

The two both laugh for a moment but an awkward silence falls upon them,

"You should probably, go now."

"Yeah, I guess so... Thanks again, for everything. Sorry, you saved me but I don't even know your name."

"Tim, my name's Tim."

"That's a nice name," she smiles softly at Andrews. "It's the same as my brother's."

*

Back in present day, Detective Tim Andrews arrests his stepfather after he confesses to raping his sister 10 years ago. He denies murdering her or having any knowledge in regards to her disappearance.

Shortly after his stepfather's prison sentence, Andrews finds a blank envelope on his doorstep. He opens it to find a small handwritten note.

'I'm okay, I'm happy, I'm proud of you. – L'

THE DEVIL'S DELICATE FIREBRAND DARLING

Sioux Jordan

My name be Rebecca West and Elizabeth Clarke be known by me from my Friday prayer meetings. She tell me what has befallen her in Colchester Castle dungeon, accused by Master Hopkins and Master Stearne of witchery, and beg me when 'tis all done with and we are freed that I should write it down being the only one who had any kind of schooling.

*

Elizabeth Clarke, was the nearest neighbour to Master Hopkins, and him not liking a beggar in such close proximity, was determined to be rid of her. She was aged eighty-one, had but one leg, no teeth and lived in a dark, damp hovel, being just one room with a smoking fireplace, a bed, a broken down table and some chairs, keeping her cats and dogs under the same roof as herself.

Elizabeth Clarke tell me herself, at one of the Friday night prayer meetings, that one night, when she be calling in her cats and dogs that Master Hopkins was passing on the lane next to her house and that he had shouted at her, that one of her dogs had tried to attack his hound.

Not long after, Master Hopkins and other righteous men of the parish of Manningtree took Elizabeth Clarke from her house, telling her the Magistrates, Sir Harbottle Grimstone and Sir Thomas Bowes, had given permission for her to be taken to Colchester Castle dungeon for interrogation by 'watching and keeping' as she was suspected of witchery. She did wail most pitifully as she was dragged forth.

I heard Master Stearne, sneer to Master Hopkins, "True and strange effects have been produced by watching and is a great means under God to bring witches to confession."

Hopkins replied, "The denying of sleep is most fitting, and is pressed for in Essex and Suffolk by the Magistrates, because they, being kept awake for days on end, are the more eager to call their imps to their help in open view, which have so happened oft times, and seldom did any witch complain for want of rest while in our keeping. The suspect should also be extraordinarily walked til their feet blister and bleed, for when they are `suffered to couch', to scratch the watchers and to hearten the witches do the imps appear immediately."

Elizabeth Clarke had never before been south of Manningtree and had heard tell of a Castle at Colchester and thought it to be some bountiful place, yet before her stood the most ruined of buildings. Having been dragged to the top of some twisting steps the fearful stench from below hit her nostrils as she descended, much worse than any house she visited; a smell of fear, human bodies and waste, rotten flesh and dampness. As she put out her hand to steady herself, her stick being denied her, she could feel the slime upon the walls and running of water.

On her arrival there, held in the dungeon, in all some twenty-five women, most so affeared they dare not speak nor tell to her their names. Not five days after Elizabeth Clarke was taken did Master Hopkins and Master Stearne bring down in to the dungeon Anne West - my widowed mother, Helen Clark - the mason's wife, Elizabeth Gooding - a labourer's wife and Anne Leech a widow, members all of my prayer meeting.

For three days and four nights she was not allowed to sleep and nor were the women already down there, crushed as they were into two small rooms, and even though the darkness made them needful of sleep. One mouthful of water and small piece of stale bread, given by the Gaoler just before he ate his fill of hot meat and bread washed down with ale, is how she counted the days. Some of the women were fearful skinny and had the foulest muck running from their bodies, as they had been there weeks, even months afore her.

At times there were as many as ten men watching them, shouting outlandish things and banging stout sticks on the walls if they thought sleep was upon them. They were made to walk barefoot on the ragged stone floor 'til their feet bled and were covered in blisters; tearing strips from their clothing to bind them, which the Gaoler soon removed. The Gaoler beat them to keep them moving so that the skin would break where not covered with their clothes. Elizabeth Clarke saw women fall and die where they stood and then be dragged out by the Gaoler by their hair, the hair oft ripping off their heads and the foulness leaving a trail.

Master Hopkins made her stand in front of him and Master Stearne, and berated her so that in the end she believed his words were true.

"Elizabeth Clarke," said Master Hopkins, "I say all witches are bad and ought to suffer, and are all alike, being either open or implicit in league with the Devil, and so I declare that all witches be in league with the Devil and should die. I have seen you, Elizabeth Clarke, with your vile sect of witches, in my home town of Manningtree and in other towns nearby, and every six weeks on a Friday eve carrying out solemn sacrifices to the Devil.

"I have seen you, Elizabeth Clarke, calling your imps to come to you and saw you speak with them, one of whom attacked my hound. You have been searched by the witch-prickers, who for many years have known the Devils marks and found also your imps teats by which they are fed, and which honest women do not have. I myself used my own needle to test your Devil's mark and you did yield no pain."

Elizabeth Clarke feared she would perish from the beatings or from getting the 'foul muck' and so, to make it stop, she confessed that which Master Hopkins wanted to hear.

"I, Elizabeth Clarke," the words came from her unbid, "confess to having lain with the Devil for six years past. He came to me four or five times a week and stayed for half the night, in the likeness of a handsome man – a man more handsome than yourself. I say that Anne West, Ann Leech, Helen Clarke, Elizabeth Gooding and Rebecca West be also witches."

She told Master Hopkins and Master Stearne, "If you be ready and will stay I will show you my imps."

Hopkins asked of her, "Elizabeth Clarke, will they do us harm?"

She replied, "No! What? Do you think I fear my own children? I will call my white imp if you will stay and have it on my lap."

In a short while they all saw an imp that appeared like a white dog, with red and sandy spots, very plump and with very short legs. "His name is Jamara," she said.

Then appeared a greyhound with very long legs and the head of an ox. "His name be Vinegar Tom. The next will be a black rabbit, named Sack and Sugar and will come for you Master Stearne and tear you. If you be not quick, my imp will jump upon your throat, and if by chance he tears your throat, then there will be toads a feasting in your belly."

An imp appeared as a white polcat with a large head and jumped in her lap and vanished as quickly. "I have five imps that be mine and two imps that belong to beldam West, now here in the dungeon. Sometimes my imps suck from the old beldam and sometimes the old beldam's imps suck from me.

I was not allowed to be quiet or to rest by the Devil until I did consent to the killing of Robert Taylor's horse and the hogs of Mr Edwards, both of Manningtree."

Master Stearne turned to Master Hopkins and spoke in a booming voice, "The nature of women is more credulous, they are commonly impatient and are apt to be misled. What makes them 'fit instruments for the Devil' is that, when displeased, they are much more malicious."

Elizabeth Clarke's confession was taken on Tuesday 25 March 1645, Lady Day, First day of New Year. I was taken to the dungeon some days later by Master Stearne and was confused and feared at seeing Master Hopkins there, a look of hatred on his face.

*

I, Rebecca West, having told Elizabeth Clarke's tale must now lay down the part my testimony took in the finding of her and others guilty of witchery.

Master Hopkins, having been known to me carnally for some seven years, visited me in the dungeons of Colchester Castle more than once, always alone and seemingly without the knowledge of Master Stearne, giving Godly comfort and instruction. He told me that if I confessed to witchery and named the members of my prayer group as witches then I would not be hanged, serve time at the Castle or be imprisoned at Chelmsford.

I stood before the Earl of Warwick, a Puritan soldier, at the County Assizes in Chelmsford and told of my confession to witchery.

"Elizabeth Clarke be our leader and we met at her house every six weeks on a Friday eve. My mother - Anne West, Anne Leech, Helen Clarke, Elizabeth Gooding and I, be all witches meeting together to seek our revenge by making a pact with the Devil. I took the Oath and Covenant, denying my Saviour Jesus Christ and God, and swore to keep secret all I did see and hear and was told that, if I did reveal that, I would endure worse torments than in hell.

"We instructed our imps on our desires and what deeds we needed them to do. Elizabeth Clarke requested her imp to scare the horse of Richard Edwards so he would be thrown and killed. Elizabeth Gooding requested her imp to revenge her accusation by Robert Taylor that she had killed his horse. Helen Clark requested her imp to kill a hog. Anne West requested her imp to free her of all her enemies and that she would have no trouble. Anne Leech requested her imp to injure a cow and I requested that my imp lame Prudence Hart, who later suffered a miscarriage.

"Half a year later the Devil came to me as I readied for bed saying he would marry me, he had the likeness of a young, handsome man, and promised if I was his, he would do what I desired and take revenge on my enemies. The Devil, taking my hand, walked me round the bedroom, and spoke the words of a marriage ceremony, I take you Rebecca, to be my wife and promise to be your loving husband until death and keeping you from harm. I responded, I Rebecca take you as my husband and promise to be your loving and obedient wife until death. I have lain with the Devil for seven years."

Despite the outcry by Master Stearne and due to the word of Master Hopkins, I procured a reprieve from being hanged. Elizabeth Clarke, Anne West my mother, Anne Leech, Helen Clarke and Elizabeth Gooding were found guilty of witchery by their confessions, my testimony, the finding of the Devil's marks, teats to feed their imps, the testimonies of Master Hopkins and Master Stearne and were sentenced to be, and were, duly hanged within four months at Manningtree.

It means that I must now leave my home town and move far away, where I am not known by face or reputation. That I need change my name, find a way to make a living and ask for forgiveness for my sins every day for the rest of my life from my mother and my friends, who I gave up for an empty promise and to save myself from the gallows.

A RECOLLECTION

Benjamin Scott

I make way through the streets of Colchester and think about time.

Yes, there are the ancient ramparts, the listed buildings, the castle that was once a temple. A historic space with subterranean secrets. But I do not think of these things. I think of the time in which I have known Colchester. My lifetime, from birth to adulthood.

I remember my Mum taking me to the doctor's surgery on North Hill to be inoculated for measles, mumps and rubella. I was quite a calm child and showed a stoicism beyond my years as the bespectacled doctor hesitantly jabbed the needle into my arm. I was quiet and accepting of the discomfort. Even afterwards, as we ambled toward the town centre, I did not make a fuss about the mark in my skin and the sharp lingering pain just below my right shoulder. So my Mum, generous soul that she is, offered to buy me a present for being a good boy.

We went into a shop on Culver Street West and upstairs to the second floor where the toys were. And there, in a box on the shelf, was the reward. An Ecto-1. Wow. The vehicle that the Ghostbusters parked in their fire station and rushed around New York City in when they got a call to catch supernatural phenomena. I had the action figures at home. Finally, I had the car too. What an amazing reward it was.

Mum had the Ecto-1 in a carrier bag that I could not stop looking at as we exited the shop and walked back on to Culver Street West. I was both excited and satisfied, filled with a kind of innocent, tremulous contentment that maybe you can only feel when you are that young. Then Mum decided that we would have a short rest so we headed into the Spoils department store in Culver Square where there was a café for customers. What was special about that café was its décor. There was an Alice in Wonderland theme, with large model white rabbits and mad hatters peering down at you as you sat there with your tea and scones on the rich dark wood tables. And the beautiful tall windows looked out on to Head Street, where the impressive post office building loomed over the pedestrians and the flow of traffic. A little rain began to pour, but that didn't matter.

There, with my mum and the magical characters and the Ecto-1 in the bag and the tasty fruit scone dressed with butter, I was happy.

I still have the car and I still have the needle's scar. I still have Mum and I still occasionally go to the North Hill Surgery. The rest is gone. The shop, Spoils, the charming restaurant, the old post office. All gone.

Yet more than this, on the same street where my precious Ghostbusters toy became forever part of my most treasured memories, there is now a different scene. There is a Starbucks coffee house, a Gap fashion outlet and, nestled in between these businesses, an Ann Summers sex shop selling toys of another kind.

Am I the only one who finds this to be a bizarre combination? I suppose it is assumed that shoppers these days must want to pick themselves up a Caramel Macchiato or a Mocha Cookie Crumble Frappuccino, buy a pair of ridiculously priced but beguilingly trendy jeans, and, while they're at it, pick up some lingerie and possibly a dildo. That is the Colchester of today, my friends. An impractical locale that obviously thinks that we have all developed an acute fondness for anything bourgeois, frivolous and mildly pretentious.

What a shame, then, that I couldn't care less about these things. Just as I am not obsessed with mobile phones, even though mobile phone centres are everywhere. Just as I am not fond of pissing in public on the High Street or falling into a booze bus to be rescued, even though the lovely late-night rising urinals and drop-in mobile medical service for drunks would seem to indicate that I am.

Do I seem old-fashioned or judgemental for a man in his twenties? Can I not appreciate the character of contemporary Colchester because I romanticize the past? Or is it simply that I am blinded by the tawdry blandness of this town and unable to see past the slow and dramatic disfiguration that has marred it? The changes, it seems, have been largely tedious, silly or seedy and have not added to the atmosphere.

For a town to be exciting I believe it must possess a certain balance of mystery, prosperity and idiosyncrasy. These qualities make us become constant tourists and we feel as though it is always an adventure to be in an area no matter how long we have lived there. We want to explore and roam, visit old haunts and try new ones. Modern Colchester does not have this effect on me, and many Colcestrians that I know are of the same opinion. Sadly, this has been the case for some time. It has degenerated into something common and uninspiring, catering mostly to the average consumer. Overwrought in some ways, run down and ramshackle in others.

While the town formerly known as Camulodunum does have an extraordinary history, this should not be its only redeeming feature. We need more investment, more unique, down-to-earth but sophisticated venues to go to. Less homogeneity. Less acceptance of social decay. We can enjoy foreign cultures and brand names without always kowtowing to big business. We can enjoy our food and drink and clothes and sexuality without having rows of the same franchises on our streets dictating our tastes for us. We should cultivate distinctiveness and decency instead of creating an environment that, were it not for its distant past, could be a hundred other places in the UK or even abroad. If I were asked to answer whether Colchester is better or worse than it was fifteen to twenty years ago I would say it is worse, but more than that, I would say it is strangely uninteresting. And decadent. It does not represent me, yet I am one of its sons. It has become a disjointed sprawl with the odd island of real culture and interest here and there amidst it.

I wonder what the future holds.

A PEACEFUL PLACE

Emma Chesters

She wanted to meet me in the café in the centre of town, in the small road off Head Street. Said we could talk over a cup of tea. She asked what time would be best. I said 8.30, before my shift started.

I walk the two miles from the hostel. Next to me I see people rushing, everybody rushing somewhere. To work, to school, so many people, all of them so busy. My pace is so slow and steady. I am too tired to rush now. I have spent most of my life moving about and maybe will again but for now I am here, in this moment, enjoying the calm and I am not racing anywhere.

I walk into the café. There are a few people sitting there enjoying their breakfasts, but I don't see a woman on her own. Would she be on her own? I don't know what she looks like. She sounded gentle when I spoke to her on the phone. Sympathetic, kind, straightforward. Can you recognise these qualities in a person's face? I sit at a table in the corner of the café. A waitress comes and I order a cup of coffee. She asks if I want breakfast. I shake my head. "No thank you." My stomach churns and gurgles in protest.

"Oh, actually, um, how much is two slices of toast with butter please?"

"£1.20."

I decide to forego some of my daily budget. It will be worth it. I am nervous and don't want my mind distracted by my empty belly. I should have eaten before I left my home but was too wound up wondering what this meeting would mean.

I look up at the café's walls, covered with photos of celebrities who have eaten there. I don't know too many of them, but one I recognise from a programme I sometimes see on the TV at the laundrette. This programme, a soap opera, has a lot of shouting, a lot of angry men and women with many problems. I wonder why people want to watch people who are so angry and who are always arguing. This country produces writers and musicians who tell of great loves and amazing adventures, but people like to watch these angry little people in a box.

A woman walks through the door and she looks around. I rise to gesture to her but she walks to a table where a man stands up and kisses her. I sit down and carry on staring at the photos on the wall. The waitress brings me my coffee and toast. I thank her and immediately start eating. I didn't realise how hungry I was. The coffee warms me.

I feel a tap on the shoulder and jump. I turn around quickly.

"Dee? I'm Jane. I'm sorry if I frightened you." The woman is in her mid to late thirties. Yes she looks kind, sympathetic and straightforward. I told her I was called Dee; my real name is too difficult to pronounce.

"Oh no." I stand up to shake her hand. "No. I was just." My words peter out. At times like this, my English becomes muddled. The waitress returns and Jane ordered a tea, milk, and no sugar.

"Shall we just start then Dee? I'm afraid I have a lot of questions for you. I will be writing notes, OK?"

"Yes OK." I nod.

She sits a little closer to me and asks in a low voice, "And you are OK talking here in the café? Because we could go to my office?"

I answer with a shrug. "No, here is fine." I try not to show my panic. I don't want to go to her office. I want to be here where there are other people around. She may look kind but appearances can be deceptive. I have learnt that lesson in the past.

"Right." she says. "How old are you?"

"I think, 24."

Her eyebrows rise. "You think?"

"Yes. I don't know for sure. I have no birth certificate. I just know I was around 4 when my family were killed."

"And that was 20 years ago."

"Yes." I nod. "About. There is a lot I don't know about myself. I don't know my birthday. I don't know the name of the village I came from or exactly where in my country. I have heard my country's name mentioned on the news here a lot. It seems war, poverty and hunger have always thrived there."

"And what happened to you in that country?" Jane is staring at me intently.

"My family were all murdered when I was very young. I know I was very small, because when the butchers burst into my home, I remember I was sitting comfortably on my mother's lap. She was singing to me. My father was sitting, chatting, at the table with my brothers and sisters. My mother was stroking my hair as she sang and then out of nowhere, these men, masked and carrying huge guns, burst through the door. They shouted. My father stood up immediately and they shot him first. Then they shot my siblings. My mother didn't scream. She just whispered for me to be still. Her back was facing them and they shot her in the head. Her body covered me and the men didn't see me. They ran out of the house shouting jubilantly. I cuddled up to my mother for many hours, eyes closed, I whispered incessantly, begging for her to get up, to help Daddy, and my siblings. But eventually I opened my eyes, saw the blood and realised I was in danger and I had to get away. I knew my family had gone forever and that was terrible, but some primitive urge in me to survive eventually made me get up and run for my life."

Jane is not showing any emotion but still staring at me. She asks me what happened next.

"Some people came, they had been friends with my parents. They had survived by some chance. They took me with them. We just kept running. I had no idea if there was anywhere to go. I just knew I needed to get somewhere else. We ate berries, drank from puddles or streams and slept under bushes. One of the people got sick and they had to stay in the next place we came to. They asked some other people there to take me somewhere safer and they did. I was so small I had to rely on adults at all times and some were very good people and some were very bad.

"At the next town we came to, I was very lucky, a family took me in. They sent me to school, fed me. I must have been with them for maybe four years. Then soldiers came and burnt houses down. People fled and I hoped to tag along with my new family. But they had six children of their own. I couldn't expect them to take me too. It was too hard."

Every time I remember this I want to cry. I remember my foster mother's face and she was so sad when she said I would have to find others to travel with. I notice Jane is sipping her tea. I didn't recall the waitress bringing it to her.

"Eventually we went from village to town throughout our homeland but the war was everywhere. We had to leave. We travelled across continent and country trying to find somewhere where we could stop running. Somewhere we could just be. Somewhere we could find peace. Some found it sooner than others. I found it hard to settle. I suppose I was still looking for my home. I know now I will not find my home but I have discovered some kind of peace."

Jane looks around the café and then back at me. "Here? In Colchester, have you found some peace?"

"Yes," I say. "I live a quiet life here. Nobody bothers me."

"Do you have friends?" Jane asks.

I think about this question. "Friends? No I don't have friends but people say hello and smile. I don't want to get any more involved than that. I can't get close to anyone. When I arrived here I did not expect to stay. It just happened. There is no conflict here, no uprisings, no political unrest, but I must be ready for this, always ready to flee. Personal attachments make this harder."

"So you don't have a wife or children?" Jane asks.

"No. I would never bring a child into this world." I raise my voice and an elderly gentleman turns and looks at me. This is something I really hate, to draw attention to myself. I shrink down in my chair.

"Where do you work Dee?"

"I work where I can. Building sites, farm work, factory work."

"What do you do when you're not working?" Jane is writing quickly. I wonder what she is writing.

"I like to walk around the town and out to the countryside. I like that Colchester is such an ancient town. The history interests me. I look at the Roman wall and wonder how many hands have touched it since the stones were first laid. I walk from one end of town to the other. Only in the daytime. I don't like the town at night. People get so drunk and there is fighting. I don't know why they fight. They are out having fun but then they get angry. I think there must be problems here but you can't see them. People aren't starving and there is no war but still they get angry and drink and fight. When I first came I was terrified of the soldiers but people tell me not to be because they are here to protect us. But those who killed my family were soldiers. It is difficult to know who is on your side. I have to go with my instincts. They have protected me all my life."

"Do you want to stay here?"

"Yes." I answer her firmly. "Yes. I would very much like to stay in Colchester."

Jane looks at me intently. "What about returning to your homeland Dee? How would you feel about going home?"

I look out of the window of the café. It has started to rain outside. It is raining hard. The greyness of the sky is washing over the street. There is no one rushing by now.

"I do not have a homeland. I have no family so there is no heart there. I do not know if I would have enemies there or if I would have any friends. It is just a place where terrible things happen. All over the globe there are places like this where terrible acts take place, day after day.

"There have always been people fleeing like me. Probably there were people doing just that, here in Colchester at the time the Romans built the wall. People have been running from danger since time began and this always will be the story for some."

Jane thanks me very much for meeting her. She says she has enough notes. She has calls to make and people to see but she will be in touch with me very soon. Her face doesn't reveal anything. I look into her eyes to try and see what is reflected of me but she blinks slowly. She puts the notes into a black leather bag and leans forwards to shake my hand. She stands, pushes in her chair and walks slowly towards the door. I look around the café and into the street beyond. The rain has stopped and people are back rushing up and down, dashing here and there. The actors on the wall are smiling down on me. I don't want to leave here, where I am warm and safe. I wonder how long I can remain.

ISAAC PALFREY - 1646

Jim Cooper

Isaac picked at the green lichen on the window ledge, rubbing the green slime between his fingers. He hated the damp that seeped into the mortar and blocked the gutters with debris either living or dead. He slipped his knife beneath a long slab of moss and sent it tumbling down eighty feet.

He watched it slap against the masonry walls and scatter in a shower of fresh streaks over the general filth that had been thrown from the walls.

Below where the last of the scattered moss had fallen, a stray dog trotted past startling the black crows that continually pecked for food amid the detritus of the castle keep. They lifted from the dirty soil, settling on the stone buttresses until the dog had passed, then fell once more to scratch at the ground to feed their bodies of feather and bone.

Despite the damp of the western facing walls, this was Isaac's preferred side to the castle. From here you could see up river across the town towards the ancient burial sites of the old Saxon kings. His roots were here, bound up in the castle walls, as was the ivy and iron straps that held much of it together.

His own downhill slide matched that of the keep's history. From lofty heights as Steward of the castle and respected town's Freemason, he had fallen to store man and county jailer. Accused and found guilty of selling short measures, only his status saved him from the castle cells.

Now he worked in the very walls his great-great grandfather had built, slopping out the prisoners and restocking the wood store for the courtroom and judge's chambers. From the bribes and favours of the cell occupants he kept alive the dream of starting out in business once more. But time was catching up on him. In his thirty-fifth year, life had beaten his heart and soul into a dark place. Losing his wife and unborn child to a fever ten years before had forced him to give his two year old to a travelling show of street performers. Better a life with them, he reasoned, than one with no mother's love.

Not all events for him, however, were bad. He had managed to hang onto ownership of his lodgings by renting them to army married couples. This brought him an income, not insubstantial, which he invested in gold; his last and remaining interest from the Freemasons. Changing times had also brought numerous rich inmates, who he could charge for extra comforts and contact with outside the castle walls.

His nest egg of precious metal became a concern; too large to conceal on his person, he took to hiding it beneath the flag stones of his guardroom over which his straw cot was pulled. This was where when the court above had an early sitting, he stayed to pull the inmates in irons from their cells to the waiting judge. These occasions were commonplace. Should a gruesome sentence be passed, it could be carried out as a public spectacle in the afternoon, sending a message to the populace to fear the law.

Isaac made his way down through the winding stone steps into the main courtyard past the main gate. Its thick door stood on rusty hinges; thick dirt and weeds at its base showing the years passed since keeping out an enemy. To the north of the courtyard, brick and tiled buildings stood beneath the shadow of the failing sunshine. Blue wood smoke rose from cook's fires, while only yards away, goats and chickens were slaughtered for the kitchen pot. Remaining chickens, goats, geese and a few sheep wandered about, little distressed by their fellows' dispatches.

The kitchen workers knew Isaac well and greeted him with gestures that he was to be served. A boy of ten lifted two deep bowls of thick stew from a table beside the cooking range and headed off toward the cells. Isaac silently went about placing breads and heavy cakes into a basket then headed off after the boy.

The steps were steep to the cells. He had to be careful where his feet fell. Walking side footed, the basket before him, he tottered down, stuffing a biscuit into his mouth and grimacing at the pain from an old broken tooth. The kitchen boy passed him half way down, taking the steps two at a time in a demonstration of youthful agility.

The dreadful smell and sound of the vaults was too much for most folk and the boy too was clearly spooked, so rapid was his ascent from the shadows and moans of Isaac's world.

The first cell reached was of better condition; a wealthy prisoner had paid Isaac for the extra space of the guard room and had tables and chairs moved in, along with wall tapestries and even portraits on the walls. The remains of a meal were scattered across a table, while the occupant lay nonchalantly on a single bed of feather mattress and tall pummelled pillows.

Imprisoned until paying off a bad debt, the man was in no hurry to be released, should the debtor be wanting to take revenge. Slowly he slipped from the mattress and made his way to the food bowls brought by the boy, ladling a large portion onto his plate.

Saying nothing, Isaac left one of the bowls and a great deal of the bread and cakes with the man. The rest of the food he gathered up and moved on into the corridor of six cells that ran three to each side under the vaulted arch of the castle foundations. No natural light filtered down here, no voices of kindness echoed from the walls, only the muffled sobs and crawling scuttles of vermin and prisoners in the dark.

Each cell was enclosed with iron bars through which food would be dropped or left just outside for the prisoner to reach if they could. In the second a woman, accused of being unfaithful, sat on a rough hewn stool trying to work at some needlework by the light of a single oil lamp. Her fingers, red and raw, bled from the needle and the tough leather that she had worked for hours.

Isaac opened her iron cage and placed the food by her feet, inspecting the piece of work on which she had spent those many hours. She had done well. The belt would fetch a good price at the town market. He slipped it through his hands while the woman ate. She would receive more sewing later in exchange for being left in peace through the long nights.

He moved to the next cell and opened the door. The wall lamp guttered at the small draught of the gate's swing. Illuminated in a corner, a young child cowered. No more than ten years old, a girl clutched at her neck line and bonnet ties. So thin were her arms and legs, the definition of bone stuck out sharply beneath the simple black cotton dress.

She was muttering to herself so quietly that Isaac became intrigued as to what she said.

"What you say girl?" He knelt beside her, his coarse tunic making it difficult to bend closer. He asked her again: "What you say girl?"

"They told me to say what she did," the girl answered him, her voice still so quiet and soft.

"What?" Isaac said, not understanding

"They asked me if mother ever turned into a dog," the girl screamed back at him. "A dog, a dog."

Primeval fear had turned the girl's face into a mask, contorting her young plump skin. She brought her hands up to her face. Her eyes revealed streaks of dry blood sneaking a path from her fingers.

Isaac fell back, his palms in the dirt. "A witch." His heart beat faster, a witch in his cells. All was possible; with a witch he could get some awful curse. Witches were bad luck and better off dead. He looked at the girl, her tear streaked face the spittle that had leapt from her lips when she had screamed at him.

He scrambled on hands and knees toward the door and swung it behind him then shook it, reassuring himself that a spell had not been placed on the iron.

To be that close to a witch, and her saying, like that, that her mother turned into a dog. He decided he was lucky to be alive.

Usually he never missed the trial of a witch. They usually gave up their dirty secrets. They died, but better a death than to live with witches casting their spells, he thought.

There must have been a trial that very morning; sometimes they went on for days. Isaac hoped he had not missed much before the burning. All witches were burnt, it killed the evil, incinerated flesh and bone. The fire's ashes were raked through by Mr Hopkins' officers and any remains cast into the river. That was the way it was; magic washed away by blood and pain.

Isaac hurried from the vaults, brushing the dust from his palms; his heart still pounding. Should there be any more prisoners, he neither knew or cared. They would be lucky to see the night out anyway in such close proximity to a child of the dark arts. He reached the debtor's cell, collected the latest coins left out for him on the table's edge and without a nod, left the vaults behind, grateful for the fresh air above.

The afternoon was half spent. There was no need to remain at the castle. He would get as far away as possible and return early in the morning for the fun.

It was a most pleasant afternoon. The parade of folk in and out of the castle gates made Isaac aware of his own rather shabby appearance. He lifted water from the horse trough and rubbed his face then ran his hands over his black matted hair and pony tail. Other wet palms of horse trough went over his tunic and twill pants. Feeling better, he left the gates behind on the trodden path into town. Two crows stood before him. One was younger than the other, its feathers were still brown and its beak was not quite the sharpness of the parent. He walked forward, expecting them to flap aside. But instead they pecked at his boots and cried out loud, their heads back until he could see the yellow of their throats. He aimed a boot at the younger one then felt a peck at his calf. He turned and looked down. A jackdaw, half the size of the other birds, had actually attached itself to his pants and was flapping madly. Not only that but five more crows were hopping toward him. One flew up to his head height in a direct attack.

Isaac scuttled along his head down and boots kicking up dust.

Soon, hot, and his breaths coming in painful gasps, he slowed and dropped his hands from over his head, expecting to feel the flap of wings but there was no sign of the birds.

Pleased to have a short cut to the sanctuary of home, he stepped left from the old Queen Street toward the Priory. The ancient brick work, covered from a thousand years of ivy, cast deep shadows as he moved through the quarter mile of wilderness. A crow flew from where he walked, disturbed from pulling at dry roots beneath the walls. Isaac jerked back, expecting another attack of crows but was pleased to see it was not he who had disturbed the bird.

A dog trotted toward him. Its coat was grey, flecked with the yellow brindle of his own cat. There were many dogs, all strays that only entertained the company of people for food and warmth of their homes.

This dog looked poorer than most, its bones stuck through its fur, making the hairs almost stand on end. One paw had evidence of a recent fight or injury as a trickle of blood had dried along the length of a fore leg. A rumble in the dog's throat made Isaac reach for a clasp knife deep within his pocket. Starting to think the whole animal kingdom was against him, Isaac withdrew the knife and held it before him, but the dog trotted inches past, brushing the ample material of his pants and then stopped, staring at him just eight feet distant.

Perplexed, Isaac walked on, occasionally turning to look behind. Three times he looked, twice the dog stood motionless, the third time the dog had gone, mingled in the shadows of the Priory.

A little unnerved now, Isaac was relieved to leave the old Priory behind and join the row of houses and church that marked the beginning of the Hythe and the port. His own property in Spurgeon Street was a source of pride to him and rightly so. In a time when three families lived in two rooms, he had real space and luxury. Although it had no water supply, it had its own privy at the end of a plot of land where he tried to grow vegetables.

Isaac let himself in through the back garden door. His army tenants lived mainly to the front and back in the two large spinning rooms and kitchen scullery. With luck, he could avoid everyone and get to his own room far above the noise and quarrelsome families below.

The stairs creaked as his eighteen stone lifted itself up the narrow flimsy staircase. The skivvy had left apples from the orchard out for him and filled his wash basin with a fresh bowl of water from the communal pump. He slumped back into an old chair stuffed with cushions set by the window. Only the sound of the drinkers in the Ale House drifted up to him. Closing his eyes, he saw the girl in the cells and the bloody birds and dog that had followed him.

Down below in the kitchen, the families were cooking the evening meal; wafts of a delicious stew lifted through the floor boards and into his room. Overcome with appetite, Isaac scoffed one of the apples but it did nothing to swage the hunger he felt.

Normally he never went close to his tenants, preferring to deal with the army agents but the smell drove him mad with longing. Not bothering to pull his jerkin back on, he went for the staircase and hand on hand rail, carefully made his way down. A woman stood in long white work dress and apron, her back to him, stirring the pot on the range. Each time her hand rotated a large wooden spoon, the smell became stronger.

She turned toward him and smiled. Isaac stood back. There was something recognisable about her, the small nose, rather large hips and silk shot back hair.

"I have come back father," she said, smiling and holding her hand out to him.

Isaac knew this to be nonsense; some sort of trick, a ruse to swindle him. He stayed where he stood, refusing to take the offered hand. His daughter had been too young to remember where she lived and the travellers were unlikely to let a fit healthy woman go.

"Who are you?" he demanded. The woman dropped her hand, her face becoming serious.

"O but I am Beth," she said. "True dead this last three years but me still right enough."

"Nonsense," he retorted. "Prove you are a spirit then."

"Then eat," said the woman, pouring stew in a bowl. "Eat and see the future and everything that is true."

Isaac's mouth watered with the anticipation of the hot meat and vegetables that formed the thick broth. On the table, fresh bread added to the compulsion. Just one feed he thought then he could report this trickster to the army and be rid of her.

He sat filling the spoon and taking great mouthfuls of the bread dipped from the bowl. He could not speak and had to listen to the woman that now stood by the door. "Why did you do it father? Why give me away to those people? Could you not have lived for me? I would have surely died for you." Isaac tried to explain the responsibility of a child scared him but the formality of eating stopped him.

Never before had he had to really think why he did such things. Usually he considered he was tough and didn't need affection and family. This was the first time he realised he was scared. Pausing for a moment, he glanced up at the woman and then turned, checking the corners of the kitchen. Only the eight sleeping bodies of the tenants gathered round the range were there.

He returned his gaze back to his plate and pushed it away in disgust. Cockroaches from the dying embers of the range heaved the stew from beneath its surface. Fury filled Isaac. What tricks were these? The sleeping bodies around could not be blamed and his inattention, that the woman had escaped, frustrated him further.

He left the cockroaches and the tenants to their night together and made his way back upstairs. Invitingly, his mattress lay uncovered. He lowered himself down on it, still cursing. Hours passed in fitful slumber until something made him wake; there was something with him in the room.

*

A sound, so soft, came from the far corner, like a rustling in the forest; something too small to be seen. Rats often came in winter to steal scraps from the kitchen but this was different-more human.

Isaac tried to raise his head but sleep had stolen his power to move. Only his eyes could roll, straining to catch sight of what troubled him. Numbed and disabled, he lay listening, trying to will movement into his body. All he felt those first terrible seconds was a gentle weight lean against the edge of his mattress.

His heart missed its beat as, looking down, he saw the white hand of a small child laying on his bed cover. Cold and white, he fought for control of his limbs, to back away to force himself from under the sheet. The small hand sought for his own beneath the covers then entwined its own soft flesh with his own pulling him away from the bed.

Isaac could see what tormented him now. It was his daughter, but little older than when he had left her at the market all those years ago. She smiled at him kindly. Her cheeks glowed with health, her skin had become warm, her clothes fresh and crisp.

"Where are we going?" He asked as his strength returned and he found he could sit upright on his bed.

"We are going to run with witches," she answered. "You are to meet my family; the people you left me with, who cared for me when you left. We shall run beneath the moon and cast magic to take on forms of other life. I shall show you, father, how to life forever."

Beth pulled him to the window. Before him lay his garden, not as he knew it but in shades of grey in one dimension as a picture on a wall. He lay his hand on the window, feeling the reality of the glass. He rubbed his eyes to restore vision but only the fur of a paw brushed his nose. A scream escaped his lips but only a howl broke into the night as he padded on all fours down the stairs and into the night.

Outside, the dog from the Priory waited for him. Panting, excited by the prospect of running the town, its tongue already hung from the saliva crusted teeth. It came as no surprise now to find Beth too had taken on the shape of a dog. Whippet like she sprinted off in front only waiting seconds for them to follow.

Their gait was fast; Isaac found what joy it was to run so light and agile. Freed from his large body and straining lungs, he went faster and faster, keeping up with the other two.

Following the river from the Hythe, ducks and swans scattered from their roosting places amid the reeds as they approached. Poachers and Gamekeepers cursed the three dogs for disturbing the still of the night as they waited for prey of their own.

Reaching East Mill, a solid line of housing kept them running close to the buildings looking for tit bits left by foxes beside the compost heaps of small holdings. They found nothing so with raised appetites sought out the grander of the Officers' mess and the barracks guardhouse. They trotted with Isaac to the fore, now complete in his persona as a dog, enjoying the freedom of living without hate or fear. He lived for now without malice or prejudice.

Finding their fill at the soup kitchen of the troops was easier than penetrating into the barracks. Treated as vermin, chances of being shot kept them out of site. Chewing the crusts of stale bread left outside the canteen window, they moved on.

As an animal, Isaac did not reason with a signal that urged him back to town and the castle keep. He just followed his instincts that led him there. But once, however, he stood before the earth ramp and bridge that led to the main gate, he wondered why so many other creatures had gathered there also.

Wolves from the forest gathered before a hundred crows and a great number of rats tumbled over unfortunate mice that ran in waves from under the castle bridge. The vermin ran in a circle of blackness until they piled up in a cone from the ground.

Solid and real, the cone rose, forming a brim five feet above Isaac's own head. Below, the whispering trail of a whirlwind reached to the ground. It spun until a shrillness whistled through the night, forcing the animals to crouch in respect to nature's force.

Witcheeesss, witcheeeesss, the wind screamed rising in pitch, piercing into Isaac's skull. Cruelllttyyy.

Isaac put his fingers to his ears, trying to quieten the wailing banshee but nothing could deaden the noise; it filled every crevice of his being. Exhausted, he flung himself to the soft ground of the earth moat and the noise vibrated around him as an ant on a drum. He lay that way listening to the earth; a higher power of witchcraft that lived through the world.

As the noise died away, he became fearful and looked about him for the face of Beth. He could put this thing right. Far more power had been shown to him that night than he knew to be real in the world. Beneath his hands, the earth was cold and wet. He rubbed his face and got to his feet. He must enter the castle and save the girl before Matthew Hopkins' men came to interrogate her again.

Another death in the name of witches must not happen, he had spent time with them, felt a freeness not of this world. He was one of them.

Hurrying across the moat, some people recognised him and shuffled aside at the roughness of his appearance. Torn and besmirched with dirt he dashed on down into the cells with a few inquisitive souls following on. Removing his keys from the hole in the wall he started to unlock all the cells, lastly reaching Beth. Her body was very still and he lifted her to his chest. She weighed nothing at all, just a wisp of leaves as light as feathers.

Turning from the cell, he collided with his first pursuer. He was a scary sight, carrying the child, and his chasers moved back against the walls.

Sprinting up the steps, his feet began to slip on the dusty stones but he never lost grip on the child's body, holding it to him. From the cells to the castle tower the cry went up. "He's a witch, burn him! Burn him!"

He was almost too fast for them. He did reach the river and fall into its embrace. He watched the bundle of rags float away before the first yeomanry guard took hold of his clothing and pulled him to the river bank.

Soaking and beaten, Isaac was bound to a pole of ash and marched to a stack of faggots. The mob was to have its way before the Witch finder was in town; the case was proven. As a dog Isaac had bound across the moat and into the cells. There, he had released the prisoners and taken the child witch to the river, where they had escaped on the water without breaking its surface.

Each time Isaac fell with his pole lashed before him, his heart grew weaker, a pain filled his chest and ran down his arm. Vomit filled his mouth and dribbled from his lips then ejected in a torrent around the assembled crowd. Scared of being infected by this witch's bile the crowd stepped back, watching Isaac die.

But he did not die alone. A dog reached forward and licked his mouth where the dribble ran and the birds descended to clear what was left after the vermin had finished with him. He was too good to leave for normal men.

Post script

Isaac's house was eventually taken over by the army until it burnt in a mystery fire during the civil war. His gold is, I think, still under the stone floor in his cell.

THE GREAT COLCHESTER TROLLEY CHARIOT RACE

Dominic Sheppard

It was cold in Culver Square after the sun went behind H and M, so we all went over to that Firstsite. Except it was cold there too, and too many fucking wannabe dudes on skateboards all over the place. Making a racket. Most of them falling over all the time too, twats. I was like, what is that about?

So we wandered up the side road by that other little gallery, towards Castle Park. But none of us wanted to go round there really. Full of dicks. Moody fucking wankers in black jumping around in their big hoodies. We don't go near them. So I didn't mind when Olly and Caz stopped and checked out the trolleys.

There was three shopping trolleys, from Sainsbury's. Someone had left them at the side of the lane. They were joined together with those little chains. Olly tried to get them apart by shoving, kicking and wresting, but it didn't work. Made a prat of himself.

"Pity," he said. "There's three of them. Six of us. Two to each trolley. We could have had a race."

"Still could," said Caz, sucking noisily on her roll-up. "We just need to put a pound coin in two of them."

"I've got a quid," said Mat.

"Me too," said Tom. He changed the spliff to his other hand and pulled a coin out, mixed up with chewing gum and a tissue. What was he doing with a tissue anyway? Dick.

"Yeah... nice one Tom," said Olly. "Wicked. Game on. What about you, Emz?" He raised an eyebrow, the way he did when he wanted to look fucking smart or something.

"I dunno," said Emz. She flicked her nice shiny hair back from her face. "Whatever."

"What do you think, Shep?" said Olly. "Fancy a run?"

I was like, "Yeah, go for it."

"Down East Hill?" said Tom.

"No fucking way!" said Emz. "Are you mental?"

"I dunno," said Olly. "Could be a laugh." He started getting the trolleys apart. Properly this time. He should have been used to it, what with him collecting them from the Asda car park on Saturdays.

Emz wasn't happy. "No. Fucking. Way!" she shouted. "Do you want to get killed?"

Caz laughed at this. "Yeah, she's right really. I mean, fuck that."

We trundled the trolleys to the end of the lane and looked down the hill. Tom passed the spliff to Caz, and she passed it to me. I had to admit, the girls had a point. There was no fucking way I was going down there on a shopping trolley either.

"Fuck it then," said Olly.

"Nah, wait a minute." I passed him the spliff, and put my hand up with one finger in the air, like Mrs Timebomb at school. "We just need to choose our route. Be creative. You know, get a little track worked out."

Emz rolled her eyes and chewed her lip. The rest looked at me like I was some fucking alien or something, but Olly was smiling, like he knew what I might say next. That might have been the spliff though.

"How about, yeah," I started and pointed vaguely towards the castle, "we go up there and we do a few side roads and stuff. We can still go all the way down and come out by the bottom of North Hill. Just won't be a massive fucking suicide mission."

Olly was smiling, but I still think that was the spliff. Mat and Tom looked at each other and nodded. Caz cackled like a witch. Emz was still looking moody but that could be Emz, like, any time.

I felt like I was on a roll. "So, right, yeah. We start from the top of Museum Street, round the corner. By that funny snooker club place. Then first left. Follow that long, then we'll come out onto that other road that goes down…"

"Stockwell Street," said Mat.

"East Stockwell Street actually," said Caz.

"Yeah, that one," I said, getting back in again. "Then follow that round. Could be tricky, but we're cool, yeah? Left, then right again, and then it meets Northgate Street. Let's do a sprint there. Up Northgate, round the hairpin by the park and then back again down St Peter's Street."

"Couldn't we just go in the park there?" said Emz.

"What for? Where's the fun in that?"

"I dunno," she said. "Just saying."

"Nah, sod that. Go down St Peters Street. Then we get to the bottom of North Hill, yeah?"

"Is that the finish?" said Olly. "By that Turkish place?"

"Oh no way man," said Tom. "We're going to need chips. I'm bloody starving."

"Chips!" shouted Caz. "And pizza!" She threw the end of her roll-up away and pulled a bottle of blue WKD out of her bag.

"Yeah right," I said. "We go up to that big red tyre place, yeah? Then over the bridge. Then Domino's is the finish. First to Domino's."

"Yeah," said Olly. "Let's do it. Just like the fucking Romans." Nobody else said anything.

So there were six of us, two to a trolley. Olly and Caz were together, of course. Olly was going to steer. Emz went with Tom, coz he was the biggest and that was the only way she was going to do it if she had to sit in the trolley. That, and loads more deep tokes on the next spliff.

Which left me with Mat. We glanced at each other a few times before he said, "I'll steer, yeah?"

"Fuck off," I said. "Not a chance. I'll steer."

He bottled it. "OK then. You'd better be fucking good."

"Easy," I said. "Done it before, innit." That last bit was a lie, but probably made Mat feel better. You can't have someone behaving like a twat in a shopping trolley, thinking like they know better or something when you're trying to steer, can you? Make them think you know what you're doing. Safe.

We all marched up to the start of Museum Street, looking like proper dicks with those trolleys and got shouted at by some wankers by that Clowns place, but I didn't give a shit. We all swigged on the WKD and passed the second spliff around again. Finished it in no time. I mean, I was fucking shitting myself really.

Turns out it's Maidenburgh Street I meant to start from. Like I'm meant to know everything. The cobbles put us off a bit, but the paths at the side were concrete, so that was cool. We lined up, like prats. Me and Mat in the middle. Olly and Caz to the left, Tom and Emz to the right.

"Who's going to say 'go' then?" said Tom.

"What do you mean, fucking 'go'?" I said. "Whoever says it will have a head-start, innit."

"I know," said Caz. "When the bottle smashes."

"Eh?" said Olly.

But she'd drained it already anyway, the greedy cow. She did her witch-laugh again and skied it. Mental. It came down all right, just missed my head, and smashed. People jumped. Real people, that is. Not us. We were off.

In the middle, I had the cobbles to deal with. Head fuck. Olly jumped it anyway and was on the pavement already so I had to follow him. No option. Tom and Emz were on the other pavement. She was making noises like someone was giving her head.

We picked up speed. The wheels fucking jumped around like nobody's business. Mat starting chanting, "Whoa, whoa whoa..." I grinned, gritting my teeth, felt proper evil.

Olly was going too fast already, the knob. There's a big fucking white arrow in the road, pointing left. "Turn, turn!" I shouted. He saw it too late. Tried to get some grip and turn the trolley, but his Converse were crap for that. He only just managed to hold it from going straight over the road, onto the paved bit and into the bollards.

On the other hand, I somehow managed to pull of some kind of fucking ballet manoeuvre, whirled the thing sideways, took the weight and surged left. Mat was quiet, although his knuckles were bright white, good lad. Tom also got it right, swerved onto the road now the cobbles were gone and ended up nearly taking my trainer off, the wanker. We were neck and neck going down William's Walk. I'd forgotten it was No Entry, but neither of us let up down the narrow alley. We both jeered at each other as the wheels rattled.

That left into Stockwell Street was a bastard. Up the curb and through some bollards there in front of some old house. Emz was lighter than Mat to push, and Tom had the inside line, the bugger, so he got way ahead. He was laughing down the hill again now, but the spliff seemed to be wearing off for Emz.

"Stop!" she shouted. "Stop! Stop! Please!" She couldn't handle it.

Tom wasn't stopping. Neither was I. We juddered over the brick path, slewing left and right again. Behind me, I heard a crash as Olly didn't make the turn and went straight into some metal gates. There was a scream, and then some laughs, so I guess they were OK, but that was the end of the race for them.

We burst out of the lane and back onto the road again. The hill was getting steeper.

"Argh!" shouted Mat. "Careful, you fuck!"

I gritted my teeth, and then the next turn came up. It was so tempting to go straight on and try the path through the flats and houses. But fuck it, a route was a route. Tom's mastery of the trolley was supreme as he dragged it left, you had to admire him.

From there, we had a nice easy slope to the next right-hand bend. We'd forgotten about the paths at this point and stuck to the road. At the end, we were meant to Give Way. But, you know, what the fuck? We were in trolleys. We just went straight out, leaning perfectly into the curve, and I heard a car screech and a horn blaring out. Fucking hell. Hadn't they seen people having fun before?

It was a bloody bumpy road as well. Tom was pulling way ahead. Emz was crying now in the front. Mat hunched his shoulders in our trolley. "This fucking hurts," he said. I mean, what was he expecting? Should have sat on his coat. Dick.

The road forked right. Another No Entry sign, another total dedication to the race. We all knew Northgate Street was coming up and then there it was. Straight run. No hill. Tom had the advantage again the bastard. With just a girl to push, he was racing away.

We got the end and that hairpin. Had to pull up to avoid a buggy, but no sweat. Back down St Peter's Street. I almost gave up then and there. Tom was too far ahead now.

But he got complacent, didn't he. I carried on chasing, made a racket, trying to put him off. He didn't think about the traffic at the end. Lights changed. Left a car standing on the crossing, and he only went straight into it, like a prick. Love it.

Emz went catapulting out onto the bonnet, and the trolley made the most massive dent in the side. Epic fail. Me and Mat couldn't believe our luck.

We weren't going to hang around though. "Go! Go! Fucking go!" shouted Mat.

And I went. Up to the red tyre place. Past the bus stop. Just missed a dog and another buggy. We chucked the trolley in the river from the bridge and just fucking legged it to the finish, both of us panting like bastards.

Only the two of us made it to Domino's in the end, but fuck it, what a laugh. I got a pic on my phone to prove it.

PATINA AND PALIMPSEST

Tom Graves

How do we talk with time?

Talking with distance is easy: we just walk. Talking with height is a little harder, with the climb, and then – worse – looking down from the heights. But time? That's something else again...

This is the oldest recorded town in Britain, they tell me. Sure – I don't doubt it. But where is time itself here? That's the hard part: that takes some looking for.

It's not in the clock on that wall above the shop halfway down the High Street – that's been stuck at ten past twelve for more than twenty years. And whilst the double-clock on the Town Hall opposite does show the right time – most of the time, at least – these days it no longer strikes the hour. A literally quiet loss – as if the town itself has forgotten its own time.

Yet that time is still here, visible, just about, in the textures around me, in the... what's the word I'm looking for? Patina – that's it. Patina. And palimpsest: that's the other word, an old parchment erased and re-used – a sadly accurate term for so much of the present-day town.

Patina is history in the usedness of things. The grain in the wooden floor beneath my feet, small dents and scuff-marks everywhere from chairs and still-ubiquitous stiletto-heels; the sway-back roofs and wobbly window-lines of the old weavers' houses in the Dutch Quarter; the comfort of an old overcoat.

I stand at the 'hole in the wall', the still partially-complete remnant of the Roman gate into the west side of town, and reach out to touch a piece of narrow red-dust tile that forms part of a line of reinforcement at waist-height all the way through the eight-foot-thick wall. Like everything else round here, it's somewhat battered, somewhat broken, yet still doing its original task, to hold up the wall and guard the gate. As I touch it, hints of time drift past: the jingle of tack, the gentle slap of iron mail on leather, the creak of a wicker-basket laden with market-goods; and behind it all, that so-subtle reek of the overcrowded town of Camulodunum. Returning to the Colchester of now, all I can sense is the stench of diesel-fumes, linked to that howl of traffic on the Balkerne Hill bypass carved across the old highway mere metres from the ancient gate; and the quiet entreaties of the magazine-seller to each passing pedestrian to buy his Big Issue. 'The past is a different country: they do things differently there' – true indeed. Yet the present is a different country too: and in some ways just as alien.

Leaving the gate, I pass beneath Jumbo – the tall old water-tower, another proud technology of another past age, now disused yet still dominating every view across the town. 'Jumbo' itself is the tiny brass weathervane way up at the top of the tower, styled as an elephant that apparently once visited the town. It still works, though the direction-pointers beneath it are somewhat out of line. Moving downward, the verdigris of the metal roof; the dull red-ochre of the water-tank itself; and the dull red Colchester brick of the pillars, stained with long streaks and spreads of dull-green algae. Dull in dullness: it's still here, the tower seems to say, still standing, yet doesn't quite know why. As if to reinforce this, the tower is surrounded now by shabby once-white wooden hoardings, put up perhaps no more than two or three years ago, yet already decrepit: they won't last much longer. A different kind of patina, this: the patina of forgottenness. Sad.

Over at the far side of town, I come across a warning-sign, mounted on another old stone wall. 'S: shelter', it says, in bold sans-serif letters. It's left over from the Second World War, hurriedly placed there when the bombs first started to fall upon the town. But the wall behind it is a relic of a much older war – the largest of the castles built by the Normans after their conquest of the country nine hundred years before. And the shelter-space beneath is the reason why that castle was built here, and built so large: its foundations are the undercroft of the vast Temple of Claudius built by the Romans to celebrate their recovery from the rebellion of Boudicca, a thousand years earlier again.

Layers of history. Literal layers of history, here: a six- to twelve-inch layer of ash everywhere beneath the town provides a forceful reminder that Boudicca was no mere myth. Her culture destroyed, her people enslaved, her daughter casually raped by a Roman soldier: by the time that wrathful warrior-queen had wreaked her revenge here, there was nothing left above the ground, and no-one left alive. Nothing Roman left intact anywhere north of the Thames, in fact – hence why the capital of Roman Britain shifted from Colchester to London once the military machine of the Romans had finally mopped up the last remnants of that rebellion. A people enslaved, again, and yet again, in so many different ways, throughout the subsequent centuries.

Another not-so-myth is up here too: Humpty Dumpty. It was the nickname of a squat iron cannon mounted by the Royalist defenders high up on the tower of St Mary's Church, beside the town's west wall, during the siege of Colchester in the Civil War of the 1640s. A cannon-shot from Cromwell's soldiers disembowelled the bell-tower; Humpty Dumpty fell down with it, and was smashed to pieces – and with it the crown's defences broken too. More patina: the tower rebuilt, yet with different brick, different pattern; history in concrete form.

That patina of history is everywhere around the town, once we know where and how to look. A small plaque beneath the gable-end of a mediaeval-style building halfway along Head Street, now a recruiting-agency but once a bakery that burnt down somewhen in the days just before the Victorian era, taking much of that part of the town with it: the plaque records yet another rebuilding. Over to the east, beside the now-silted river that once made Colchester a serious sea-port, lead bullets still embedded in the wooden beams of the Siege Mill provide another tangible reminder of the town's turmoil in the Civil War. And in the centre of town, amongst the older buildings, often all we need do is look above the current shop-line: evidence of pride, of care, of workmanship, is everywhere displayed.

Yet suddenly, some few years before the First World War, it all stops. A sudden nothingness. Decoration all but disappears on all new buildings; pride and purpose replaced, it seems, by the relentless pursuit of whatever paltry profit could be gleaned from other people's lives. A change of religion, perhaps: the old church at the far end of the High Street erased to make more room for the market, the old temples replaced by banks and other new temples of the religion of money. Yet even that overt grandiosity of greed seems forgotten now: those banks are just another tawdry type of high-street shop, another empty soulless space distinct from others only by the minor differences of corporate signs.

It's notable that of those few grand old houses tucked away in the hidden side-streets of the centre of the town, almost all are now owned by lawyers – perhaps because their work must needs connect with time? Elsewhere, though, not so much a loss of history, as no sense of time at all: the patina of the past obliterated often by intent. History as palimpsest, it seems – place as parchment not so much re-used as rubbed-out, erased over and over again until there's almost nothing left.

That's all too true of the so-called 'pedestrian-friendly' shopping precinct in the centre of town. Two gaping holes clawed out and concreted over, either side of the core heritage area, around the square-towered Saxon church and the beautiful Elizabethan splendour of the now-abandoned clock-museum at Tymperleys. Two holes punched through the southern part of the Roman wall, to make space beneath for heavy trucks to haul consumer-goods for those 'exciting' new consumer-stores. Thirty years on, those stores too have their patina, of sorts: but unlike the old buildings, they don't wear well. Tawdry faux-'heritage' fittings tacked together out of cheap timber fall apart, paint flaking off in so many all-but-inaccessible places, exposing the emptiness beneath; everything looks tired now, the fragile fabric of the superstructure, supposedly so expensive, now shows itself only as expensively cheap in the worst sense of the word.

All these shops that need such bare emptiness of space within them to sell, sell, sell; yet for all their glitter, so many of those precinct-shops – especially the smaller ones – are empty now, closed, abandoned, gone. Having no space for soul, the soul departs: and that soullessness pervades so much of elsewhere in the town, as in so many towns' central spaces. People still struggle up the Scheregate steps each day, or push their prams through the somewhat gentler slope of St Johns Wynd; but at night all those small shops along Sir Isaac's Walk and Eld Lane, balanced on the edge of the Roman wall above those ancient gates, are closed and shuttered now, the only sign of life there some occasional piece of litter blown along by the bleary eastern wind. An empty world, celebrated only for the vapidity of its showy shallowness: so dependent on the sellability of the shallow 'new' that it must needs always hide from any hint of old.

Yet as with every palimpsest, the signs of life before can still be found. People do still care enough that street-signs scattered here and round explain what once was there. And times connect, weave through each other: out near the edge of the eastern precinct, beneath what once was the coach-yard of the centuries-old Red Lion Inn, the archaeologists uncovered a far older Roman mosaic that did indeed depict a lion, in delicate lines of fine red-orange stone. It's there still, mounted on a side-wall of a shop in Red Lion Yard: or a copy of it, rather, because the original mosaic is now safely tucked away in some museum – the kind of place where history goes to die.

But at least it still exists, that mosaic: that's something, some tangible link with past. And with the future, too: perhaps that's the real point here. We have records in the ground of the Roman past, and of the culture that preceded it that was its equal in everything but warfare. We have written records going back ten centuries and more; drawings and engravings from at least half that time; and photographs too that in some cases date back almost two centuries now. But our own time? – not so sure. Librarians warn us that this could well be a generation that erased itself from history: emails and electronic images are easy to handle now, yet could vanish in an instant – and without a museum to maintain the means to read them, there may soon be nothing left at all. An empty palimpsest, erased by accident: perhaps not the greatest gift we could leave to future generations...

So where is our own patina now? Where do our footsteps register within the history of the town, other than in the fake-flagstones of the shopping-mall? As we sweat our way up North Hill's steep slope, how do we connect with those who did the same in times past, and will do the same in time future too? Can we see amongst the cars of now the horse-carts of the past that somehow made it up the slope without sliding back? Can we sense the foot-traffic and perhaps-strange-to-us vehicles that will contend with that same steep climb in some future time? What patina will we bequeath to them from our own usedness of this world?

Your choice, the trees stretched out above me seem to say, as I make my way beneath them on the quiet walk home, away and onward from the town.